"There's something out there."

Alice spoke with a surety and finality that worried Jill.

"We don't have *time* for this bullshit." Peyton pushed past Alice and proceeded down the alley.

"No," Alice started, but Peyton didn't listen.

Just as Jill was about to join him, the report of dozens of rounds being fired at once slammed into Jill's ears—

—just as the cause of those reports slammed into Peyton's form. Blood splattered as the bullets tore through his body, and he went flying backward.

He was dead before he hit the ground, which he did about six feet behind where he was standing.

"Peyton! No!"

Jill looked up as a figure stepped out of the shadows.

"Figure" was truly an inadequate word. The person was at least eight feet tall, with huge muscles, tubes running in and out of his flesh, was carrying a big weapon that was roughly the size of Texas, and wearing a rocket launcher slung across his back.

"Nemesis."

RESIDENT EVIL: Apocalypse

A novelization by Keith R.A. DeCandido
Based on the screenplay by Paul W.S. Anderson
Based on Capcom's bestselling video games

POCKET STAR BOOKS
New York   London   Toronto   Sydney

This book is a work of fiction. Names, characters, places and incidents are products of the author's imagination or are used fictitiously. Any resemblance to actual events or locales or persons, living or dead, is entirely coincidental.

An *Original* Publication of POCKET BOOKS

A Pocket Star Book published by
POCKET BOOKS, a division of Simon & Schuster, Inc.
1230 Avenue of the Americas, New York, NY 10020

ISBN: 0-7434-9349-4

First Pocket Books printing September 2004

10 9 8 7 6 5 4 3 2 1

POCKET STAR BOOKS and colophon are registered trademarks of Simon & Schuster, Inc.

Manufactured in the United States of America

For information regarding special discounts for bulk purchases, please contact Simon & Schuster Special Sales at 1-800-456-6798 or business@simonandschuster.com.

To Marco,
for more reasons than
I'm willing to admit in public . . .

ACKNOWLEDGMENTS

Special thanks to editor Marco Palmieri, who dragged me into this; agent Lucienne Diver, who kept me in it; author S.D. Perry, who did all the other books; writer Paul W.S. Anderson, who provided the source material; the game developers at Capcom, who provided Paul's source material; GraceAnne Andreassi DeCandido, who kept my writing sound; and my super-duper wonder sweetie Terri Osborne, who keeps me going.

ONE

Major Timothy Cain didn't take any shit.

He'd been born with a different name in Berlin back when the city was separated by a large wall. The third of four children, and the youngest boy, he had the misfortune to be on the wrong side of it. Shortly after Mother died, when he was sixteen, Father had managed to secure a way for them to emigrate to the United States. Upon arrival, Father had declared their name to be Cain—an anglicization of their name in German—and gave all his children new names. They were now Michael, Anthony, Timothy, and Mary, because those, Father said, sounded like American names. Anytime they used their old German names, Father would hit them until they stopped. Not being fools, all the children learned quickly to think of themselves with their new identities.

In gratitude to his new home, Timothy enlisted in the army on his eighteenth birthday. Shortly thereafter, he was sent overseas to fight in the Gulf War. Father was happy that his son did so. Michael, who was three years older than Timothy, had moved to Chicago and become a police officer; Anthony had moved to San Francisco and lost touch with the rest of the family. As for Mary, though women could serve, she had no interest in doing so, preferring a career in business.

Timothy Cain became alive for the first time in the desert. He had always succeeded academically, but mostly by rote. He was a fast learner, but he had never had much enthusiasm for it. The two years of school he'd attended since immigrating were difficult, since Timothy spoke with a thick German accent, which made him the target of teasing by his peers, and made it difficult for him to derive any kind of enjoyment from the learning experience.

Combat, though, he took joy in that, especially when that combat was against the enemies of the United States of America. And in the desert, nobody cared about his accent, except for a few idiots, and they all shut up once they saw Timothy Cain in action.

It didn't take long for him to distinguish himself, work his way up the ranks. He was leading his fellow soldiers into combat after only a few weeks, and his men would follow him anywhere. He had a natural charisma, an aptitude for tactics, and an especially fine ability to kill Saddam's foot soldiers. Subject to the usual armed forces proclivity for obvious nicknames, he quickly became known as "Able" Cain, because no matter how bad the mission, no matter how ridiculous the plan, no matter what it was you needed to get done, if you put Sergeant Timothy Cain in charge, it was going to get done. Period.

Cain learned many things in the desert, but the most important thing was that, contrary to what Father had always taught him, life was neither precious nor sacred.

Life was, in fact, cheap.

If life was such a glorious, magnificent, wonderful thing, then it wouldn't be so easy to take it away.

If life was a great gift, then he wouldn't be able to kill a fellow human being with one hand, as he did often in the Persian Gulf.

When his tour ended, he went to officer candidate school to get his commission.

After several more years as an officer, he realized another important truth: there was more to life than the military.

That truth didn't so much come from plowing through the desert and blowing up the enemy, something at which he had frankly excelled. No, this truth came from the gentlemen in suits who worked for the Umbrella Corporation and recruited him to run its Security Division. Able Cain had served his country. In a sense, he would still be doing so, for Umbrella had many government contracts and provided services for Americans everywhere.

The main difference was that now he'd be recompensed with an obscene amount of money.

Having achieved the rank of major, Cain said yes to Umbrella's proposition, though he insisted that he still be referred to by his rank. He was also able to buy Father a house in Florida. When Michael was shot in the line of duty, and afterward was going slowly insane at a desk job, Timothy made him the head of security for Umbrella's Chicago office. He tracked Anthony down in a crack house in Berkeley and got him cleaned up, paying for his detox. (That he later jumped off the Golden Gate Bridge was hardly Timothy Cain's fault.)

When Mary learned her husband was cheating on her, Cain paid for her divorce lawyer. Then, after the divorce was finalized and Mary had taken the bastard for all he was worth and then some, Cain tracked the ex-husband down—living in a shitty little studio apartment in South Bend, Indiana—and shot him in the head.

Life was, after all, easy to take. But it was so much more satisfying to destroy someone first.

Now Cain stood outside the mansion. Located in the neighborhood of Foxwood Heights, two miles outside the Raccoon City limits, the mansion looked like something out of one of those snooty British movies that Cain hated rather than an actual structure outside a small American city.

It was also owned by the Umbrella Corporation, used as the primary entry point to the Hive.

Five hundred men and women employed by Umbrella lived and worked in the Hive, a massive underground complex where the corporation's most sensitive work was done.

The existence of the Hive was not kept a secret—it was impossible to sequester five hundred employees, many of whom were in the upper echelons of their respective fields, without someone noticing they were missing—though it was not widely advertised either. Umbrella kept its public headquarters in downtown Raccoon where everyone could see it: the public face of the company that provided the best computer technology and health-care products and services in the country.

Unfortunately, something had gone horribly wrong in the Hive. The facility's sophisticated artificial intelligence—named the Red Queen—had gone quiet, security measures were activated, and the Hive was now sealed. Cain had sent a team led by his best security operative, a Special Forces veteran who went solely by the code name One, to find out what the hell had happened.

In that, they seemed to have failed, since their contingency plan—sealing the Hive—had been enacted. That only would have been the case if the team was incapacitated or killed.

Cain had assembled a team of doctors and security personnel outside the mansion as backup for One. Based on the protocol that the Red Queen appeared to have used, the crisis was medical in nature and the AI had felt the need to activate a quarantine. So the entire team was dressed in Hazmat suits, with several gurneys and diagnostic equipment on standby, and a sterile umbilical linking the entrance of the mansion with the helicopter that would take them back to Umbrella's Raccoon City corporate headquarters.

Observing the feed from the security cameras located throughout the mansion on his PDA, Cain and his team waited to see if anyone would emerge from the Hive.

Only two people did. The first was the head of the Hive's security, Alice Abernathy, one of Cain's top people. The other was a man Cain didn't recognize. Of One and his six-person team, there was no sign.

That was bad news. Not only was One Cain's best operative, but the team he'd brought were Umbrella's elite. Bart Kaplan, Rain Melendez, J.D. Hawkins, Vance Drew, and Alfonso Warner were the best of the best, and Olga Danilova was a talented field medic. If they were dead . . .

Still, Cain felt no trepidation, because Cain hadn't felt trepidation since he enlisted in the army. As a teenager, sure, he'd felt trepidation all the time—his skin was breaking out, he'd struggled with the language, he had difficulty with girls—but once he reached the desert, he never feared anything again.

Because he knew the secret.

Life was cheap.

As Cain watched on his PDA's screen, Abernathy and the man made it to the vestibule just inside the mansion's front door.

The man had three wounds in his shoulder that looked like they were made by large claws.

Cain instantly knew what had happened. Someone—probably the fucking computer—had let the damn licker out.

This was turning into a clusterfuck of epic proportions.

Abernathy stumbled to the floor. She was carrying a metal case, which she dropped. The wounded man knelt next to her. Abernathy was crying.

Crying? What the hell had *happened* down there to make a professional like Abernathy *cry?*

The camera had an audio feed, and Cain turned it up. Abernathy's voice sounded tinny on the PDA's small speaker. *"I failed. All of them. I failed them."*

Cain shook his head. It looked like everyone was dead.

One of the security people asked, "Should we move in, sir?"

Holding up a hand, Cain said, "Not just yet."

"Listen," the wounded man said, *"there was nothing you could have done. The corporation is to blame here, not you."* He indicated the case that Abernathy had dropped. *"And we finally have the proof. That means Umbrella can't get awa—"*

He cut himself off, wincing in pain.

Cain smiled. From the sounds of it, this guy was some kind of crusader. How the hell he'd managed to infiltrate the Hive was something Cain would worry about later. From the looks of things, this asshole was about to find out just what those wounds really meant.

The jackass kept talking. *"—get away with this. We can—"*

Again, he cut himself off.

"What is it?" Abernathy asked.

7

The man screamed, and fell onto his back.

"You're infected. You'll be okay—I'm not *losing you."*

Cain had seen enough. "Let's move in."

Two members of the security detail opened the door and proceeded inside.

Abernathy shielded her eyes from the blinding light that suddenly poured into the vestibule. "What's happening? What're you doing?"

One guard reached for her, while the other, along with one of the medics, knelt beside the crusading moron, who was now convulsing on the floor.

"Stop!" she yelled.

Cain sighed as she fought off the guard with a few well-placed punches. Something obviously had happened to her down there that had a profound effect on her personality—but it didn't have the least effect on her fighting ability. She was still the best.

Even as the wounded man was loaded onto one of the gurneys, three more of the guards tried to grab Abernathy. It took her maybe five seconds to subdue them.

Damn, she was good.

"Matt!"

So that was the guy's name. Cain looked to see that this Matt person was growing tentacles out of the three wounds in his shoulder.

Definitely the licker. And this might turn out to be just what they were looking for.

"He's mutating. I want him in the Nemesis Program," Cain said.

Maybe they could salvage *something* out of this fuckup.

It took about twice as long as it should have, but the guards, with some help from a well-placed syringe full of sedatives, finally managed to put Abernathy down. She kept screaming Matt's name.

Again, Cain wondered what the fuck had gone on down there.

He checked the case Abernathy had been carrying. It had room for all fourteen vials of the T-virus and the anti-virus, but several of the vials were missing. That didn't bode well at all.

"I want her quarantined. Close observation, and a full series of blood tests. Let's see if she's infected. Take her to the Raccoon City facility, then assemble a team. We're reopening the Hive. I want to know what went on down there."

One of the medics, a pissant little twerp whose name Cain didn't give enough of a shit about to learn, said, "Sir, we don't know what kind of—"

Cain didn't have time for this. He needed information, and the only way to get that was to go into the Hive. "Just do it."

Abernathy and this Matt person were loaded onto the helicopter. The head of this security detail, a former Marine named Ward, gathered up his people.

"Ready when you are, sir," Ward said, sounding singularly unenthusiastic.

"Something bothering you, soldier?"

"I'm not even supposed to be here today." Ward's

face was hidden behind the mirrored faceplate of the Hazmat suit, but Cain could hear the smirk in his voice.

"Tough shit. One's down there somewhere; it's up to you to find out what happened to him."

"Due respect, sir—if they took One out, we ain't got a snowball's chance in hell. Moving in, sir," he added quickly.

Only those last three words saved the ex-jarhead from a tongue-lashing. Ward could be a real whiner, but he did his job. Today of all days, Cain didn't want to put up with his usual shit.

Armed with MP5Ks and all looking alike in their white Hazmat suits, the seven-person team moved through the high-ceilinged rooms of the mansion in a moderately tight formation. One of them—probably Schlesinger; that little punk was always slow—kept lagging half a step behind the other six. Cain brought up the rear.

Ward signaled another of his people—Osborne, the tech-head in Ward's team, recognizable by the sterile bag of tricks tethered to the belt of her Hazmat suit—once they reached the giant floor-to-ceiling mirror in the sitting room. She opened a panel with two knob switches, revealing a socket. Reaching into her pouch, she pulled out a plug and inserted it.

The mirror slid open to reveal a concrete staircase. Osborne then pulled out a minicomputer and started tapping its keyboard with gloved hands. "Sir, I still can't access the Red Queen. I should be hardwired into it now."

"Try again."

Osborne tapped more keys. "Nothing, sir." She looked up, her mirrored visor staring at Ward's equally blank visage. "The only way this could be happening is if the computer was totally fried."

"One's team was supposed to shut down the computer and remove the memory."

"They did more than that—if it was just that, I'd be able to restart her in at least a limited mode. But there's nothing there to fire up. The Red Queen's dead."

Cain ground his teeth. Definitely an epic clusterfuck.

He gave Ward a nod, and Ward then signaled his team to move down the stairs to the bottom, where the way was blocked by a giant blast door.

This, Cain knew, was the contingency plan in action.

It was about to be put into inaction.

"Open it."

Ward nodded, then gave another nod to Osborne, who entered more commands into her minicomputer.

A second later, the blast door opened.

Ward and Schlesinger took point and moved in, MP5Ks at the ready. The rest of the team followed, with Osborne and Cain himself bringing up the rear.

Two seconds later, Cain heard the scream.

Only after the scream did he hear the footsteps.

He hadn't realized they were footsteps at first; they were so rhythmic that he assumed them to be the background noise of the Hive's operations. But no, these were feet moving slowly and meticulously.

Osborne pulled a flashlight out of her pouch and

shined it ahead just as the sounds of gunfire erupted ahead of Cain.

Ward was shooting into a crowd of people. Next to him, Schlesinger lay on the floor, his Hazmat hood removed, a huge hunk of flesh ripped out of his throat.

As usual, Schlesinger was too fucking slow.

Ward kept firing, but even as the bodies fell, more kept coming. There seemed to be an endless supply of them.

"What the fuck *are* those things?" Osborne asked.

Cain said nothing, but simply looked at them. All of them were wearing either dark suits or lab coats over all-white outfits. Said clothes were filthy and muck-encrusted, but still recognizable as clothes conforming to Umbrella's strict employee dress code.

That wasn't why Osborne had asked her question, though. No, it was the faces.

At best, they were blank and expressionless.

At worst, they were missing parts.

One person's neck was at an impossible angle.

Another's throat was almost completely missing, only an exposed spinal column keeping head attached to body.

Another was missing both eyes.

Another, its cheek.

Many had wounds on their bodies—teeth marks on some, bullet holes on others.

The four hundred ninety-two employees who lived and worked in the Hive were all dead.

And, based on the fact that this was not stopping

them from wandering around the Hive, they had been killed by the T-virus.

Which was doing exactly what several of Umbrella's top scientists had predicted it might do if it went airborne. Especially after those experiments in the forests by the Arklay Mountains. Umbrella had managed to hush up that particular nightmare, and then moved the project down to the Hive, which could be contained in case of a disaster.

At least in theory.

Even as Ward and Clark went down, overwhelmed by the tide of dead Umbrella employees, Cain was wondering how this might have happened. Most likely, some overeager asshole had decided to steal the T-virus and the antivirus. Abernathy and her friend Matt, maybe? Impossible to be sure.

The gunfire continued, but the ones that had been shot at the start of the fighting were now getting up. One of them leapt onto Shannon and bit right into his left arm through the Hazmat suit. Heddle, panicking, shot both Shannon and his attacker, and the pair went down. The attacker got right back up and leapt for Heddle, as did a brown-haired woman in a lab coat.

Osborne had pulled out her Beretta and ran into the crowd, firing away.

Waste of time.

For his part, Cain turned and walked back up the stairs. Ward's team would keep the creatures occupied long enough for Cain to evac.

Abernathy hadn't struck him as the opportunistic

type, but maybe someone had made her an offer she couldn't refuse. God knew there were enough people out there who wanted to get their hands on the T-virus.

Cain heard the screams of Ward's team as they died one by one. Perrella, Kassin, and finally Osborne all went down.

They had served their purpose. Cain now knew what had happened in the Hive. That was all that mattered.

Life, after all, was cheap.

TWO

The air-conditioning still wasn't working.

Randall Coleman, Raccoon 7's news director, didn't think it was too much to ask that the AC function. True, it was fall, but all the equipment they had in the control room needed to stay cool.

But when the AC broke down last week, management hadn't made it a priority, given the time of year.

Then the heat wave hit.

The whole thing was maddening. They'd get temperatures in the nineties, then it would dip into the fifties when the sun set. Half the staff of Channel 7 was out sick, thanks to the messed-up weather.

Still, they were managing. Randall's assistant, Loren Bills, had set up several fans throughout the control room, which kept the oppressive air moving and meant that at least some of the equipment was likely to keep functioning.

Fortunately, the equipment itself was quality stuff. Raccoon 7 was no rinky-dink independent that let its network affiliation carry it. Not like those snooty jerks at Channel 9, who thought they were hot shit just because they were a UPN affiliate, but mostly used that as an excuse to cut costs and staff and use substandard equipment.

Channel 7, though, was the most-watched local station in Raccoon City, and that without being an affiliate of any of the six networks. They were truly independent.

Which was how Randall liked it.

Directing the morning news on Raccoon 7 was just a stepping stone for Randall, but it was an important one. Channel 7 was a proven quantity, one of the most respected independent stations in the country, and one known for producing excellent technicians. Here, Randall could learn the craft of directing and producing.

Down the line, it would lead to work at the networks, and eventually he might be able to go freelance and direct actual TV episodes—or even movies.

True, what he did here was basically see-Spot-run directing—Camera 1 on Sherry Mansfield, Camera 2 on Bill Watkins, Camera 3 on the two-shot, Camera 4 roving. But someday he'd be able to move on, maybe direct a sitcom, or one of those cop dramas.

Randall loved cop dramas.

And eventually, he'd get his break, and finally break into films. And then maybe, finally, he'd be able to bring his masterpiece to the big screen.

Because he knew nobody would look at his magnificent screenplay, *Scales of the Dragon,* right now. Right now, he was a nobody, a guy directing morning news at an indie station in a small-market town.

But Randall was patient. Soon he'd work his way up to the top. Soon he'd be able to write his own ticket, and then *Scales of the Dragon* would be produced.

No matter what Mom said.

Right now, Camera 4 was on Terri Morales, doing the weather.

Terri had on her reassuring smile. It looked great on camera. So did the cityscape behind the anchor desk, and it was just as fake.

Her vivacious voice came through the speakers next to Randall's monitor.

"Six-ten in the a.m. and already the temperature is at a massive ninety-two degrees, as this unprecedented heat wave continues."

Dabbing sweat from his brow, Randall figured it was more like a hundred and two in the control room.

"Why do people say 'in the a.m.' all the time?"

Randall looked at his assistant. "Loren, I'm not in the mood."

"No, really, I mean, why put it there? What does it add to the sentence, except maybe a veneer of pseudo-hipsterism?"

"Clear skies, low humidity, a light breeze coming in from the west. And, as a special bonus just for you, we even have a pollen count of just point-seven."

"Just for us," Loren said, "right. Like the Fates got

together and said, 'Hey, let's keep the pollen count down *just* for the people watching Terri Morales.'"

"Loren, shut the fuck up and ready Camera 3."

"That's right—zero-point-seven! And that's a record low for this time of year. Good news for all you hay-fever and asthma sufferers. All in all, we're in for an-other beautiful day."

Loren shook his head. "She's on fire this morning."

"Yeah, too bad they don't give out Emmys for the weather. Go to Camera 3."

As Loren switched over to the two-shot of the an-chor desk, he asked, "Hey, you think they'll ever give her back the job as anchor? She's certainly bland enough."

Randall blurted a laugh. "Not in my lifetime."

Sherry and Bill were finishing up.

"Stay with us—after the break we'll be looking at your holiday hot spots."

"Stand by—going to c-break in three . . . two . . . one . . . and we're out."

"Back in sixty," Loren added.

As soon as the word "out" came out of Randall's mouth, he saw Terri Morales's face change on the Cam-era 4 monitor from perky and smiling to aggravated and scowling.

"Someone get me a fucking cappuccino before I puke!"

Even as one of the terrified production assistants ran to fulfill her request, Terri reached into a pocket and pulled out a pillbox. Randall knew that it was full of an assortment of uppers, downers, relaxants, and pep pills, none of which would be taken together by a rational, sane person.

However, nobody had ever accused Terri Morales of being a rational, sane person.

A rational, sane person wouldn't have gone ahead and aired footage of a city councilman taking a bribe that she had been explicitly told not to air until she got a corroborating source. She claimed she had one and aired it anyhow, only to have the lie revealed later, and the footage likewise as being a fake. Instead of exposing Councilman Miller as a corrupt bastard, it had made him look good while vilifying the ever-untrustworthy TV news media. It was a major black eye to Raccoon 7, which until then had a pristine news reporting record.

The only thing that allowed Terri to stay employed was the *Raccoon City Times* publishing an exposé on Councilman Miller the following week. Taking bribes was a spit in the ocean of the man's corruption, as it turned out, and while this didn't exonerate Terri, it at least ameliorated her situation. After all, the only person really harmed by what she'd done was now facing a dozen indictments.

Still, it didn't look good. One of the reasons Randall liked it at Channel 7 was that the station staff took their journalistic integrity seriously. Maybe they couldn't fire Terri without risking a backlash—not to mention the chance of a competitor hiring her—but they could demoralize her. Demote her to the Raccoon 7 weather chick.

It also made her résumé look bad for any prospective employers.

Randall was really going to enjoy it when he moved on to bigger and better things in Hollywood while Terri Morales was still talking to Raccoon City about pollen counts.

"Remember how it used to be?"

Randall looked up at the commercial that was now running on the on-air monitor. It showed a beautiful woman of a type that Randall knew didn't exist in real life getting out of bed. The bedroom was incredibly neat and snazzy—of a tax bracket Randall had long aspired to but not yet achieved.

"That fresh face that you'd see every morning in the mirror?"

The woman wiped the condensation from the bathroom mirror to reveal a gorgeous face.

"Yeah, right," Loren said, "like anybody looks *that* good first thing in the morning. Oh, sorry, 'in the a.m.'"

For once, Randall agreed with his AD. Even supermodels looked like shit first thing.

"Before the cares of the world got you down?"

Now it was the same shot, but the woman was older. Even the bedroom looked a bit more decrepit—more like a real bedroom. For that matter, the woman looked more real: crow's-feet, a few wrinkles, baggy eyes.

"Want to turn the clock back? Well, now with Renew Cream, you can. Applied as your daily moisturizer, its unique T-cell formula rejuvenates tired and dying cells."

Accompanying this was a simple graphic that showed

the cream being absorbed into the body, with brightly colored cells replacing dead skin cells.

"Christ, that's the best they can do?" Loren said. "I can do better animation than that on my fucking Mac."

"Loren, shut the fuck up." Randall spoke out of reflex.

The beautiful, not-real version of the woman came back.

"Bringing the young, fresh-faced you back to life."

"Right, 'cause heaven for-fucking-fend that you actually, y'know, *look* your age."

"Loren, what part of 'shut the fuck up' don't you get?"

A sped-up voice that sounded to Randall like the Alvin and the Chipmunks album his nephews always listened to said, *"Renew is a registered trademark of the Umbrella Corporation. Always consult your doctor before starting treatment. Some side effects may occur."*

Randall frowned. "Aren't they supposed to *list* the side effects?"

Loren snorted. "Shyeah, right."

"No, really, they passed a law or something, didn't they?"

"How long you been living in Raccoon, boss?" Loren grinned. "You oughta know by now that Umbrella lives by its own rules."

Randall couldn't deny that. Umbrella all but owned Raccoon City. Hell, one of its subsidiaries owned a piece of Channel 7. It wasn't a majority, but it was, Randall knew, enough to kill aborning more than one investigation into Umbrella or one of its subsidiaries.

Come to think of it, one of those investigations had been by Terri Morales, back in the day.

The last commercial began. "Back in thirty," Loren said.

Refocusing his attention on the show, Randall cued Camera 3, and thought about the day when *Scales of the Dragon* would get made.

THREE

"Hey, Jeremy, why's it called the Ravens' Gate Bridge?"

Jeremy Bottroff swore he was going to kill his parents.

No, that wasn't fair. It wasn't their fault—hell, they'd been kind enough to let him move back home after San Jose.

He really needed to kill Mike.

Of course, he'd have to find him first.

"Jeremy?"

Ignoring Greg's importunings unfortunately wouldn't make his teenage brother go away, so he finally answered the question. "There used to be a whole mess of ravens that lived in that little park on our side of the bridge. When Raccoon City expanded out to this side of the river, they needed a name for the neighborhood.

Since it had so many damned ravens, they called it Ravens' Gate. When they built the bridge, that's what they decided to call it."

As Jeremy spoke, he slowed his battered old Volkswagen Golf as he approached the tollbooth, grateful that his parents had also lent him their FreePass that let him avoid the toll lines. It would allow him to get Greg to crew practice that much faster, then turn around, head home—or, rather, to his parents' place—and go back to bed.

Then he could try to figure out how to fix up the mess he'd made of his life.

No, that wasn't right. The mess *Mike* had made of his life.

Jeremy hoped that wherever Mike wound up, he would die of an exotic disease. Since he was probably in a country that didn't have an extradition treaty with the United States, that was at least a possibility. Besides, Mike never paid attention to what he ate.

As opposed to Jeremy, who never paid attention to the financial side of the small business he and Mike Jones had started two years ago in San Jose.

Don't worry about the dot-com collapse, Mike had said.

Don't worry about the Silicon Alley downsizing, Mike had said.

Don't worry about our diminishing customer base, Mike had said.

Don't worry about me stealing what few profits we have left and haring off to some foreign country, leaving you to face the music, Mike most assuredly *hadn't* said.

He might as well have, since Jeremy hadn't worried about it, and it had happened.

Broke, ruined, his face in the pages of *BusinessWeek* as another casualty of the new millennium's economic downturn, Jeremy had returned to his hometown of Raccoon City.

A year ago, he'd been a big-ass tycoon. He had a staff, he had a beautiful apartment with a view, he had a girlfriend named Shawna with big tits, no brains, and an insatiable sexual appetite.

Then Mike had disappeared, along with the money, and Jeremy lost, in rapid-fire succession, the staff, the apartment, and the girlfriend. Or maybe he lost Shawna before the apartment. It had all happened so fast. At least he hadn't been dumb enough to ask Shawna to marry him.

Now he was another lame-ass business failure, living at home with Mommy and Daddy and reduced to driving his younger brother to crew practice at the crack of fucking dawn. All things considered, he could hardly have said no when his parents asked him to take Greg. They were, after all, letting him live rent-free in the house, eating their food, drinking their booze (drinking *a lot* of their booze), and taking up space in the house.

Still, things were looking up—or at least not looking down. He had an interview set up with Umbrella's human resources department. It had taken him a month just to get the HR interview—for some reason, the country's largest supplier of computer technology didn't see a man whose most recent foray into that field had ended with bankruptcy and indictments as a hot commodity—but he had it later this afternoon.

Which was why he wanted to get Greg to crew practice and get some more sleep.

Of course, if he hadn't insisted on staying up until 2 A.M. watching crappy movies on cable and depleting Mom's supply of tequila, getting up to drive Greg to crew might not have been so onerous.

But what the fuck else did he have to do with his life?

"Why'd they call it Ravens' *Gate?*" Greg asked. "I mean, it's not like it's a gate, really."

"Sure it is. It's the gateway to this side of the river and it's full of ravens." He smiled. "'Sides, they wanted to call it Ravens' Haven, but the city council said that sounded dumb."

"No, they didn't."

"What, you don't believe me?"

"No."

"Then why'd you ask me in the first place?"

"'Cause I'm bored."

"So I gotta be bored, too?"

"Whatever."

Jeremy breathed a sigh of relief as he went through the tollbooth and the sign indicated that his parents' FreePass had enough money on it to allow him onto the bridge. Greg saying "Whatever" generally signaled an end to the conversation. Since Jeremy hadn't wanted it to start in the first place . . .

It was still early enough that few drivers were on the

bridge. Past the tollbooth, the cars spread out as they achieved whatever cruising speed they preferred, making the bridge look deserted. Within twenty minutes or so, the commuters would start pouring onto the bridge in force and then it would become a still-life in vehicles.

Probably mostly SUVs, because, after all, you needed a fucking off-road vehicle to get from your fancy house to your downtown office. . . .

Like those guys.

Jeremy blinked.

What the hell—?

Just as he noticed them in the rearview mirror, Greg asked, "What's that noise?"

Greg's window was rolled down—the AC had long since died, and Jeremy really wasn't in a financial position to have it fixed—so he stuck his head out and looked up. "There's a black helicopter back there! Betcha they're from Area 51."

"Area 51's in New Mexico, wiseass."

"I'm gonna tell Mommy you said 'ass.' "

Jeremy looked again at the rearview mirror—there looked to be over a dozen black SUVs zipping across the bridge going at least seventy.

"I'm a grown-up, Greg, I can say whatever the fuck I want."

The Golf had to struggle to maintain sixty-five, so the SUVs all passed him. As they went, Jeremy noticed that they all had heavily tinted windows. Which, as far as he knew, was totally illegal.

The amazing thing was that the SUVs were bumper-to-bumper, yet still moving at about seventy. It was like fucking robots were driving them or something.

He sneaked a quick glance up to see the black copter Greg was oohing and aahing over. It was in tight formation with the SUVs.

What the fuck was going on?

The last one went by, which by Jeremy's count was the fifteenth, and then he saw the license plate. Instead of the usual random set of numbers and letters, it had a vanity registration: UC 15.

Jeremy also noted that the frame of the license plate had the stylized logo of the Umbrella Corporation emblazoned on it.

When they reached the Raccoon City side of the bridge, the SUVs all continued toward the heart of town, still in a perfect straight line.

As he continued across the bridge, Jeremy Bottroff decided he was looking forward even more to today's job interview.

FOUR

"Do you have to fucking *do* that?" Mike Friedberger asked his partner.

"Do what?" Peterson asked, sounding oh-so-fucking-innocent as he navigated the SUV through the streets of Raccoon City.

"Crack your fucking gum. I fucking hate it when you crack your fucking gum."

Peterson shrugged as he turned a corner onto a nearly empty side street. Mike wished he wouldn't shrug and drive at the same time, but he held out about as much hope of that happening as him not cracking his fucking gum.

"Tough," Peterson said. "Maybe if you didn't curse so much, I wouldn't crack my gum."

"Oh, give me a fucking break."

"Would it kill you to not curse so much?"

"Does it fucking matter? I mean, really, what fucking harm am I doing?"

Peterson smiled one of those goofy-ass smiles of his that made Mike want to punch him repeatedly in the face. "About as much harm as I'm doing cracking my gum."

"Yeah, but the fucking difference is, you cracking your gum is an annoying fucking sound that drives me up the fucking wall."

"And you using the word 'fucking' as a piece of punctuation is driving *me* up the wall, but do you hear me complaining?"

"Yeah, actually, I do."

"We're there."

"What?" Mike turned and looked down at the GPS on the dashboard. It transmitted a map of the area from an Umbrella satellite in orbit. A signal from a tiny device in the vehicle's undercarriage was sent up to the satellite, allowing the satellite's computer to add a red flashing dot to indicate where their SUV was on the map. A similar transmitter at their destination was also transmitting to the satellite, and it was indicated by a solid blue light.

All in all, the various transmissions and equipment cost upwards of a million dollars, just to do something that Mike could've fucking well accomplished by looking out his tinted window and seeing the giant house belonging to Dr. Charles Ashford, at which Peterson was pulling up.

The computer display was kind enough to tell them that Ashford was a Level 6 employee of the Science Division, and that this was a high priority extraction. All of which Mike fucking well knew, since it was why they were driving this fancy-ass SUV through Raccoon City at oh-God-early in the fucking morning.

But Umbrella wasn't happy unless they were spending a lot of money on stupid shit. That's what big corporations *did*.

As long as Mike's own paycheck cleared, they could overspend all they fucking wanted.

Now, if they could just partner him with someone who wasn't a fucking prude and didn't crack his fucking gum all the time.

Peterson pulled into the driveway, neatly placing the SUV smack in the middle and perfectly straight.

Whatever his other flaws, Peterson was a fucking good driver. Handy skill for a wheelman.

"Who is this guy, anyhow?" Peterson asked as he climbed out of the SUV.

"One of the high fucking muckety-mucks in the Science Division."

"Which means what, exactly?"

"Means he's a lot smarter than either of us, makes a lot more money, and if we piss him off, he'll give us an exotic disease that he created in his lab."

Peterson chuckled. "Got it."

"Seriously, know that wrinkle cream they're doing all those fucking commercials for? With that really fucking hot broad?"

"Yeah, I've seen them. And nobody uses 'broad' anymore."

"What're you, the fucking language police? I can't say 'fuck,' I can't say 'broad,' mind telling me what the fuck I *can* fucking say?"

Peterson cracked his gum especially loudly. "Say whatever you want."

They walked up to the front of the house; Mike rang the doorbell. "Thanks a fucking lot, wiseass. Anyhow, this guy's the one who designed that wrinkle cream, pretty much." He smiled. "Oh, yeah, you know that computer in the Hive?"

"What, that creepy little kid?"

Mike nodded. "That's this guy's daughter."

"Really?"

"Yeah. Fucking nuts, if you ask me. I mean, you really wanna talk to a fucking little kid every time you use your fucking computer?"

"We picking up the daughter, too?"

Rolling his eyes, Mike asked, "Did you even fucking *listen* to the briefing? No, Bob and Howie're handling that." Mike didn't envy his brother Bob catching that assignment. Taking a little kid out of homeroom always sucked. The teachers all got fucking indignant and the kids were all stupid, and it was just a fucking mess.

Besides, it served Bob right. *His* partner didn't crack gum in the car. Howie Stein was a good guy. Better than Mike's little brother fucking deserved, as far as Mike was concerned.

Finally, the front door opened. Mike at first thought it had opened automatically, because no one was there.

Then he looked down and saw that Dr. Charles Ashford was fucking handicapped. He was in a wheelchair.

Millions of fucking dollars of equipment in the car, a fucking briefing beforehand with Major Cain, and they couldn't fucking *once* mention that the guy was in a fucking wheelchair?

Putting on his game face, Mike looked down at Ashford and said, "Excuse us, sir. There's been an incident."

Ashford's eyes went all wide. "What?"

"You have to come with us," Peterson added.

"How did it happen?" Ashford sounded pissed.

"Sir, please." Mike said that mainly because he didn't have the first fucking clue *what* had happened, much less how. He was just going where Major Cain told him to go.

He looked at Peterson and nodded in the scientist's direction. Peterson, miracle of miracles, got the fucking hint, and went around to start maneuvering Ashford out the door.

One advantage to the guy being a fucking cripple was that they wouldn't have to argue with him too long, they could just bring the fucking wheelchair out.

As Peterson grabbed the wheelchair handles, he repeated, "You have to come with us."

"But my daughter already left for school."

Mike tried to sound soothing when he said, "It's been taken care of, sir."

Peterson wheeled Ashford toward the SUV. Mike

wondered how fucking crippled this guy was, and whether or not they'd be able to get his scrawny ass into the SUV.

Maybe Bob *had* gotten the easier assignment after all.

As Peterson wheeled Ashford down the driveway, he cracked his gum.

Ashford winced. *"Must* you do that? It's extremely annoying."

All of a sudden, Mike decided he really liked this Ashford guy.

FIVE

Angela Ashford hated homeroom almost as much as she hated being called Angie.

Unfortunately, she had to put up with both of those things every day. Everyone called her Angie like she was some kind of dumb little girl, and she *wasn't*. She was a big girl, and smart, too.

And she hated homeroom.

Homeroom was mostly annoying because it had Bobby Bernstein in it. Angela hated Bobby Bernstein. All he ever did was pull on her hair and call her names with his stupid friends and call her father a cripple.

Angela hated that.

Especially the part about Daddy being a cripple.

It wasn't Daddy's fault that he was a cripple. Or that Angela used to be one.

He had tried to help her.

She still remembered the conversation Daddy had with those men from the company he worked for. Angela wasn't supposed to be listening, but she had left her room to go to the bathroom and heard Daddy sounding upset.

Angela didn't like it when Daddy was upset.

She didn't hear everything, because she was upstairs and Daddy was downstairs in his study, but she heard enough to make her scared.

". . . you've perverted my research," Daddy had said. *"The T-cell could eradicate disease worldwide!"*

Angela didn't know what "perverted" meant, but she could tell that it was something bad.

"Then who would sign your paycheck, Doctor?" one of the other men had asked.

Later that night, she had heard Daddy crying in his room.

But Daddy still helped her. He had made her better.

For this year, Angela's homeroom teacher was a stupid man named Mr. Strunk. He had fake hair on top of his head that he kept saying was real, and he had a big moustache that was all gray and black. All the other kids called him Mr. Stunk, but that was because all the other kids were also stupid. Angela didn't like Mr. Strunk very much because he never made Bobby Bernstein and the other kids stop pulling her hair, but she didn't think it was very nice to call him Mr. Stunk, either.

Mr. Strunk was making the morning announcements. Angela tried to pay attention to them, but Dana Hurley kept whispering to Natalie Whitaker right behind Angela, so she couldn't hear a thing.

She'd liked it better last year in Ms. Modzelewski's homeroom. Ms. Modzelewski sat them in alphabetical order by last name, so Angela was always up front in the first row, right behind Carl Amalfitano and in front of Tina Baker and next to Anne-Marie Cziernewski. Carl and Tina were always quiet, and Anne-Marie was nice to Angela. Bobby Bernstein sat in the back of the row, far away from Angela.

Suddenly, the front door opened. This startled Angela.

It apparently startled Mr. Strunk, too, since he dropped the clipboard he was reading the announcements from. It hit the floor with a clatter that made Angela jump a second time.

She grabbed her Spider-Man lunchbox. Daddy had given her the lunchbox right after he made her better. Angela liked Spider-Man because he always won in the end even when he wasn't supposed to or when bad things happened to him. Daddy said when he gave it to her that he got it because she was his little hero.

He didn't put her lunch in it, though. It was something much, much more important.

The last thing her father said to her every morning before she got onto the school bus was always the same:

"Don't ever lose track of that lunchbox, sweetheart."

She always said the same thing back:

"I won't, Daddy."

And she never did.

So when the two men in the gray suits walked into the classroom, the first thing she did was go for the lunchbox.

"I'm sorry, sir," one of the men in the gray suits said, "but I'm afraid I need to take Ms. Angela Ashford out of class."

"Whadja *do*, Angie?" Bobby Bernstein asked. He stretched out the word "do" so it sounded like a dirty word.

A bunch of the other kids laughed.

Angela really hated Bobby Bernstein.

She was also scared that something had happened at home. The men in the gray suits looked just like those other men in the gray suits.

The ones who worked for the company Daddy worked for.

Angela didn't like them very much.

"What's going on here?" Mr. Strunk asked. He bent over to pick up his clipboard.

"We were sent by Angie's father's employer, sir. We've been instructed to pick Angie up."

"Is something wrong with my daddy?" Angela asked.

One of the men in the gray suits looked at Angela, then held out a hand. "Please, Angie, you have to come with us."

Angela hated being called Angie, especially by grown-ups.

"Is Daddy okay?" She refused to get up from her desk until the man answered her question.

Bobby Bernstein put on a stupid voice and repeated, "Is Daddy okay?" His stupid friends laughed some more.

"Your father's fine, Angie, but you need to come with us *right now*."

She got up, gripping her Spider-Man lunchbox.

The other man in the gray suit said, "You won't need your lunch, Angie."

"I'm not goin' without my lunchbox."

"Fine, whatever," the first man said. "Just come with us, please."

Mr. Strunk stepped forward. "Look, I can't just let some strange men walk into my homeroom and take one of my students."

The second man reached into the inner pocket of his gray suit's jacket and pulled out a piece of paper, then handed it to Mr. Strunk.

Mr. Strunk read it. His big moustache drooped as he did so.

"All right, fine," the teacher said, handing the piece of paper back to the second man in the gray suit.

The first man still had his hand out to Angela.

"C'mon, Angie, we have to go."

"Yeah, *Angie,* we have to *go,*" said Bobby Bernstein. His friends giggled.

Angela muttered, "I hope you die, Bobby Bernstein."

It was too quiet for anyone to hear—except for Dana, who gave Angela a smile.

Dana didn't like Bobby Bernstein either.

Clutching the Spider-Man lunchbox to her chest as the men in the gray suits led her out into the school hallway, Angela asked, "Where're we going?"

"You'll see, Angie."

Angela didn't think that was much of an answer.

They went out the school's front door, which was supposed to be locked after homeroom started.

But if these two men were from the company Daddy worked for, it wouldn't be the first time they'd done something they weren't supposed to.

In fact, they weren't supposed to take her out of class like that. But they got Mr. Strunk to let them do it.

She held the lunchbox tighter to her chest.

A big black car was parked on the street in front of the school, right under the red sign that said **NO STANDING ANYTIME.**

There was no ticket on the car.

Angela knew something bad was happening.

Was Daddy sick? Was she sick? Had they found out something bad about Daddy?

Or was it something even worse?

The second man in the gray suit opened the car's side door. The car was so big, Angela had to climb into it like it was a stepladder. She almost dropped the lunchbox.

Angela sat in the backseat while the two men sat in the two front seats.

"Let's boogie," the one in the passenger seat said.

"Why do you always say that?"

"Say what?"

" 'Let's boogie.' It's stupid."

"Will you just drive the fucking car?"

"Hey, language! There's a kid in the backseat."

"Fine, will you just drive the *freaking* car, then? Sheesh."

The big black car pulled out onto Hudson Avenue, heading past Robertson Street toward Main Street. Main Street was just what the name said it was: the main street in Raccoon City. Actually, there were a lot of big streets in the city, but Daddy had explained that in the old days, Main was the only big one. Now there were other big ones, like Shadeland Boulevard and Johnson Avenue and Mabius Road, but Main Street was still one of the most important ones.

The man in the gray suit who was driving was still talking as he drove down Hudson Avenue.

"Have you ever actually 'boogied' a day in your life?"

"Why are we still having this conversation?"

"Well? Have you?"

"Jesus, Howie, it's an *expression*. Haven't you ever used an expression in your life?"

"Sure, but I like to use ones that have some basis in reality, y'know?"

"It *does* have a basis in reality. Boogie is a type of dancing. Dancing is a type of moving. We need to move. It's just a variation on 'let's get moving.' "

"So why don't you just say, 'Let's get moving'?"

" 'Let's boogie' has fewer syllables."

"Oh, I get it—you're a card-carrying member of the

Society for the Prevention of Syllable Overuse. Paid your dues this month?"

"Y'know, when my wife gets like this, I assume she's on the rag. What the hell's your excuse?"

The driver neared the big red stop sign at the corner of Hudson and Main, but wasn't slowing down. "I just don't see what saying 'Let's boogie' has to do with what we've been doing, especially since you don't boogie."

"How the hell do you know I don't boogie? Have you ever been with me in a situation where I might be dancing?"

Angela looked out the window on her right. She saw a large truck driving straight down Main Street.

Driving very *fast* down Main Street.

The man in the gray suit who was driving was still talking about boogieing. He had not stopped at the stop sign. Probably, he thought he didn't have to. After all, he didn't have to follow the rules that said Angela had to be in school all day. He didn't have to follow the rules that the front door of the school had to stay locked when school was in session. He didn't have to follow the rules that said you couldn't park in front of the school.

So he probably thought that he didn't have to stop at a stop sign, either.

But the truck wasn't slowing down.

Neither was the man in the gray suit.

Until he saw the large truck.

"Jesus Christ!"

Everything happened quickly after that. Angela

couldn't see anything except the back of the seat right in front of her. It was all sounds.

She heard a squealing noise.

Then she heard a sound like a hammer hitting a wall.

Then she heard a sound like crumpling paper.

Then she heard screams.

She also felt things: like she was on a roller coaster. She got bounced around the big black car.

No matter what happened, though, she made sure that she held on to the Spider-Man lunchbox.

And as she heard a screeching sound that was just like fingernails on a chalkboard only much, much louder, she wondered if she'd ever see her daddy again.

SIX

Lloyd Jefferson "L.J." Wayne had been arrested so many times that he could practically handcuff himself.

It was almost a weekly ritual. Either he'd get nailed for some shit he was involved in, or someone else was involved in some shit that the RCPD needed the 411 on, and they'd bust L.J.'s ass on some bullshit charge so they could get him to roll.

L.J., not being a fool, usually rolled. All part of the dance.

He knew he was small-time. L.J. liked it like that. Yeah, the cops'd bust his ass, but it was never for hard time. Shit, he'd only done gone up in the joint but once, and that was only six months.

Stick with the misdemeanors, a few cheap-ass felonies, and his black ass was home free. He made some good cash, kept a roof over his head, and was his own boss. Shit, he knew what times were like. He was sellin' dope to white folks that didn't have it as good as L.J.—losing their jobs and shit, buyin' smack with their severance pay 'cause life was so fucked-up.

Today, though, today was no fuckin' day to be rotting in RCPD's cage, dog.

Today there was some *serious* shit goin' down, and this was the last place L.J. wanted to be.

All day there'd been all sorts of weird shit happening. People stumbling around like they were in some drive-in monster movie shit or something, not sayin' nothin', just *biting* people.

At first, L.J. figured it was just some crazy-white-folks shit, right up until he saw Dwayne.

Dwayne was a punk who thought he was the big nigger on the block 'cause he'd done hard time as a juvie. Least, that's what he *said*. L.J. didn't buy that shit for a minute, but he let Dwayne talk the talk, long as he paid the cash money for the goods.

Today, though, Dwayne came stumblin' up to L.J.'s three-card game. L.J. was a little light in the wallet, and it was the end of the month, which meant Junior Bunk was goin' around makin' sure everyone was all paid up in time for this month's shipments. L.J. owed Bunk two large, which L.J. didn't have on account of the fucking Colts losing to the fucking Saints, so he figured he'd take some money from some tourists. He set up a cardboard box on the corner of Hill and Polk Avenues, took out his lucky deck of cards that he stole off the newsstand at the bus station, pulled out three cards, and started shuffling.

So what happened? L.J. was takin' some mad money from two dumb-ass white folks, including one mother-fucker who thought he knew "all the tricks these people pull," and Dwayne came up all quiet-like and bit Gomer and his wife and knocked down the cardboard box L.J. was using for three-card.

What got L.J. was Dwayne's eyes. His eyes were *dead*. He was also pale and shit—his skin was more gray than brown.

Then Dwayne shuffled off, the white folks ran away screaming—*with* their money—and L.J. was left clean-ing up the fucking mess.

L.J. saw more of this kinda shit for an hour, before one of his three-card assholes turned out to be a fuckin' cop.

What really sucked ass was that this was gonna be his last one. He was still short what he needed, but Bunk could kiss L.J.'s black ass—only place he wanted to be was in his crib with his custom Uzis and the police lock on the fuckin' door.

Instead, this white detective was bringin' him in on a shit misdemeanor when there were zombies and shit all over the city.

Crazy as the streets had been getting, it wasn't noth-ing compared to what the cop house looked like. L.J.'s cousin Rondell used to talk about the crazy-ass shit that'd go down in cop houses in New York, but that sorta shit didn't happen in Raccoon.

Until today. Cops all *over* the fuckin' place, running around, shouting at each other, yelling on the phone.

L.J. couldn't make out a single word anyone was saying—just a big-ass wall of *noise*.

"Come *on*," L.J. was saying to the detective who was dragging him in. "You think anybody gives a shit about my narrow black ass right now? Look around!"

The detective just said the same thing he'd been saying since he finished reading L.J. his rights back on Polk Avenue: "Shut up." When they got to Sergeant Quinn's desk, the detective said, "Book him on a three-fourteen."

"You must be outta your minds! Look at me—I'm a businessman!"

L.J. looked around the cop house. He saw two uniforms—a cracker-ass white boy named Duhamel and his partner, a candy-ass nigger named Cooper—bringing in a big guy who looked whiter than milk.

He had the same dead eyes Dwayne had.

"Now, lookie there at that trippin' Herman Munster motherfucker. *That's* your problem."

Duhamel and Cooper were having a bitch of a time keeping ol' Herman subdued. Duhamel yelled to the sergeant, "Give us a hand over here! This guy's insane!"

Quinn walked around to the other side of his desk and moved L.J. toward the holding bench.

"Jesus!"

L.J. turned around—that was Cooper, who was now holding his arm and grimacing like he was in some *deep* pain.

"He bit me!" Cooper was yelling. "Son of a bitch *bit* me!"

Duhamel, like a typical cracker-ass white boy,

started beating on Herman with his nightstick. Fuckin' cops always went for the fuckin' stick when things didn't go their way.

Quinn cuffed L.J. to the bench, then ran across to help out Duhamel and Cooper.

Herman was taking a mad beating, but it wasn't doing shit. He just fucking *stood* there.

L.J. wasn't liking this at *all*.

"Yo! You can't just leave me here, Quinn! You gotta give me some hardware, man!"

Quinn ignored him, and whipped out his own stick to use on Herman.

Shaking his head, L.J. turned around to see who else was stuck on the bench.

There was just one woman—dressed like a ho. Probably *was* a ho. Shit, if they was bustin' L.J.'s ass, they were probably sweepin' the hos on Harbor Street, too. End of the month, Bunk wasn't the only one wanting the books clean. Cops had to answer to assholes, too—fucking quotas, so they picked on legit businesspeople like L.J. and honest hos like—

Shit, L.J. knew this one. He couldn't see her face, 'cause her head was down, practically sunk into her tits. And there was plenty of room down there, too, which was how L.J. actually recognized her.

"Rashonda? Goddamn, is that *you,* girl?"

But Rashonda didn't say shit. Was like she fell asleep or some shit.

With his free arm, L.J. nudged her in the ribs. At least he had some company.

"Now, don't be sayin' you don't remember me."

She looked up.

Only then did L.J. see that her shoulder was bleeding. Looked like somebody'd bit her.

And her eyes were as dead as Dwayne's and Herman's, and all the other zombie-ass motherfuckers he'd been seeing all day.

"Goddamn, girl, who you been fuckin'?"

Then her mouth opened a whole lot wider than any mouth had any fucking right to. Rashonda's teeth were all black—and trying to bite L.J.

"Shit!"

SEVEΠ

They told Jill Valentine she was insane.

They told her she was rumormongering. That what she was telling everyone was truth was, in fact, in the realm of video games and action movies, not real life. That she was seeing things, that she was mistaken, that she was overreacting.

Then they told her that she was suspended.

All for reporting something she'd seen with her own eyes—and shot with her own weapon.

Or, rather, the department's own weapon. Which they took back, along with her badge, when she was suspended.

Apparently, being a highly decorated officer for her entire career didn't mean anything. Helping save the mayor's life when she was a uniform didn't mean anything (well, why should it, that mayor wasn't in office anymore, and even if she had been, politicians had short attention spans). Being put on the elite Special Tactics and Rescue Squad didn't mean anything.

It should have. Her word should have meant something, especially given how high profile the S.T.A.R.S. were.

Those—those—*things* she'd seen in the forests of the Arklay Mountains were real. They really killed people. And she really had barely escaped with her own life.

But they were also linked to the Umbrella Corporation.

One thing Jill Valentine had learned working for the RCPD: you didn't fuck with the Corporation. They owned the town—hell, they owned half the *country*. You didn't mess with something they didn't want you to mess with.

So instead of heeding the words of one of its most decorated officers and doing something to protect the citizenry from these undead monster-movie rejects, the RCPD instead chose to—or, more accurately, was forced to—condemn the decorated officer as a raving loony and suspend her for filing a false report that was a hundred percent true.

And now all hell was breaking loose all over Raccoon City.

Just as Jill had warned them would happen.

She put on a blue tube top and a pair of shorts—the temperature was in the nineties on this fall day—then, after a moment's thought, put on her tall boots. At first glance, she looked like a run-of-the-mill twentysome-thing babe. In reality, she had freedom of movement for her arms and legs, and boots that could put someone down with one well-placed kick.

And Jill Valentine knew quite well where to place her kicks.

The next stop was her rec room. As she entered, she picked up the television remote, curious as to what the TV news was saying about the fact that the same mon-sters that she'd seen in the forest were now roaming the streets of the city. She was especially curious whether there was a statement from Umbrella.

The screen flickered to life, showing the happy-yet-concerned face of Sherry Mansfield.

"—ill no explanation for this wave of unexplained killings that is sweeping across the city. Husbands killing wives, children killing parents, perfect strangers attacking one another. A deadly crime spree with no ap-parent motivation and seemingly no end."

No clue. That just figured.

Jill wondered whether Umbrella was covering it up.

She looked around her rec room. One wall contained several shelves full of trophies. Most were for sharp-shooting, plus a couple for pool playing. Her eyes then moved to the regulation pool table, her lucky stick lying diagonally across the green felt, the cue ball and the eight still sitting on top next to it. She'd been hitting the balls around this morning in another futile attempt to unwind.

Above the pool table was a neon Budweiser sign.
That was a gift from Eamonn McSorley, the owner of
the bar where she'd spent a good chunk of her misspent youth hustling men who made the mistake of
thinking that this good-looking brunette teenager was
an easy mark. Once she was accepted into the academy, she'd told Eamonn that pool hustling wasn't
something she could continue to indulge in, so she
wouldn't be coming around to McSorley's Bar and
Grill anymore.

So he gave her the sign. Given the amount of money
she had brought into the place—word got around
quickly about the teenage bombshell who couldn't lose
at pool, and every asshole in town wanted to be the one
to beat her—it was, he said, the least he could do.

The two long walls of the rec room were taken up
with targets.

Each one was full of bullet holes.

Jill had been meaning to get the things replaced.
Now, though, there didn't seem to be much point.

Captain Henderson had taken her badge and her
department-issue weapon, but that didn't leave Jill unable to defend herself. She walked over to the closet on
the wall with all the trophies and pulled out a shoulder
holster and her trusty automatic.

It was the same weapon she'd used to kill one of the
monsters in the forest, after her official weapon ran out
of ammo, and after she realized that the *only* way to stop
the things was a head shot.

Luckily, Jill was good at head shots.

Holstering the automatic, she grabbed the TV remote, and switched off Sherry Mansfield's face.

She went outside and saw only chaos.

Jill owned a brownstone that she'd inherited from her uncle. The rec room was in the basement and had its own exterior door. As she exited and locked the door, she saw, on the sidewalk in front of her stoop, a woman biting a man on the arm, the man screaming.

Unholstering the weapon, she shot the woman in the head. She fell to the ground.

The man, still screaming, took a look at Jill and ran down the street.

Jill considered shooting him, too, but he was moving too fast, and she didn't want to waste a bullet in case he wasn't infected. The woman had bitten him on the sleeve of his shirt, so it was possible that the infection wouldn't pass on.

Of course, somebody *else* was likely to bite him before long.

As she walked down the street toward her Porsche—like the brownstone, a gift from her now-deceased uncle—she saw Noel in his usual spot in the alcove between the brownstone next to Jill's and the bodega on the corner.

Normally, Jill would toss a quarter into the hat Noel kept in front of his cross-legged self. Today, though, the hat wasn't there, and Noel seemed to be asleep.

"Noel?"

The homeless man looked up. His normally blue eyes were a milky white.

He also had a bite mark on his left cheek.

Without hesitation, Jill shot him in the head.

"Yo, bitch, whadjoo do *that* for?"

Jill turned to see some punk kid wearing a wool cap even though it was ninety degrees outside. His eyes were normal, and he was talking, so he wasn't infected.

Yet.

"He was already dead," Jill said. "I was just finishing the job."

"Bitch, you fuckin' *crazy*."

"That's what they keep telling me."

She pulled the keys out of her pocket and beeped the alarm, unlocking the doors to her flame-red car.

After getting in, she started the engine and checked the rearview mirror.

The kid in the wool cap was going through Noel's pockets, looking for change.

"Grave robber calling *me* crazy," she muttered as she pulled out into the street. "This keeps up, I'm gonna start talking to myself."

Raccoon City was falling apart. One minute, she'd see a scene of total chaos; the next, the streets were as empty as a ghost town. Here, a sidewalk café being overrun by undead waiters trying to eat their patrons. There, a zombie shuffling through a bus that had crashed into a storefront. Over there, a gaggle of the living dead wandering through an office building lobby.

Jill made a decision.

She had left the apartment intending to go to the station house in order to help out.

But this city was beyond help.

They'd called her crazy. They'd disregarded her testimony. They'd told her she couldn't do her job anymore.

So fuck them. They didn't want her to serve and protect, then she was out of there.

However, she still pulled into the RCPD's main HQ parking lot. She had to get a few things.

Inside, the squad room was a disaster area. Desks overturned. Perps and cops alike running scared. Zombies everywhere, some in handcuffs, some in uniform. She saw Duhamel and Cooper attacking Borck and Abromowitz. Some old drunk was attacking Fitzwallace. The sarge had managed to stay alive so far, but Quinn was presently beating off a fat man who was trying to chow down on him.

Shaking her head, Jill pulled out her piece.

Ten very loud seconds later, all the undead creatures in the room had fallen to the floor, bullets in their skulls.

Quinn looked down at the fat man's corpse, then up at Jill. "Glad to see you back on duty, Valentine."

Jill snorted and headed for her desk, which was one of the few still intact and upright.

"What the hell're you doing?"

Sighing, Jill ignored the familiar voice of Captain Henderson, who had burst out of his office. She was amazed he had the balls to actually open the door.

"Valentine! You're on suspension!"

As if that mattered. Again, Jill sighed. She opened her desk drawer and pulled out her spare automatic, a thigh-strap, and more clips. "I told you," she said, "shoot for the head."

"Why are you even here, Valentine?"

What a question to ask. As if she was no longer truly a cop.

Well, maybe she wasn't—at least, not in a town that was controlled by a multinational corporation that didn't give a damn about human life. Or on a police force where captains didn't stand up for their people and just let them get railroaded into suspensions for no good reason except to cover a corporation's ass.

"Just cleaning out my desk." She buckled on the thigh-strap, then holstered the second weapon there. She put the ammo in the pockets of her shorts.

Without even sparing Henderson a glance that, frankly, he didn't deserve, Jill headed out, this time going past the sarge's desk. Quinn had always been good to her.

"You okay?" she asked.

Quinn chuckled. "I was gonna ask you the same question. I'm thinkin' I shoulda taken that early retirement Sheila's been goin' on about. Florida's lookin' *real* good right now."

"My advice? Go home to Sheila, and then get out of town."

Shaking his head, Quinn said, "No chance. My shift ain't over yet."

Jill sighed a third time. Quinn had been on the job for almost thirty years. His father and uncle had both been RCPD, and so had his grandfather. He'd always been a little too dedicated. But she couldn't fault his loyalty.

For Jill's part, loyalty was something she had no reason to keep giving the RCPD.

"In that case, Sarge, shoot for the head. That's the only way to stop these things."

Quinn nodded. "Good luck to you, Valentine."

"You too, Sarge."

As she passed Quinn's desk, she saw a zombie hooker trying to bite an overdressed perp who was cuffed to the bench.

"Keep away from me!" the perp was screaming, even as the hooker moved closer. "Rashonda, stop it! Help!"

Jill shot Rashonda in the head. She slumped onto the bench.

Then she turned her gun on the overdressed perp.

"Oh, shit, not me!"

She pulled the trigger.

The handcuffs, and the part of the bench they were attached to, splintered and broke.

Once he realized he was free, the overdressed perp leapt up and moved as far from the bench as he could.

"Freaky gnarly-ass ho tried to eat me!" Then he looked at Jill. "And you! God*damn!* What the hell's goin' on here?"

"You carrying a gun?" she asked.

The perp snorted. "I wish."

"You might want to find one."

Then she turned around and looked at Quinn, Henderson, and the other cops still alive. "I'm leaving town—I suggest you all do the same."

Without another word, she turned and headed out.

As she worked her way toward the door, she heard the frantic voice of a uniform on the dispatch radio. Jill was pretty sure it was Wyms.

"Dispatch, we need backup—immediate backup to Rose and Main. Dispatch? Come in, dispatch. We're being overrun. Officers down. Pulling back. Help us, dammit. We need help. Dispatch! Please!"

Even as Wyms's pleas grew more frantic, they faded from Jill's hearing as she headed back to her car. They'd had their chance to stop this, and they'd blown it.

They'd told Jill Valentine she was insane.

Now the entire city was paying the price.

EİGH✝

All in all, this was the worst vacation of Carlos Olivera's life.

He'd started his stint in the air force right out of high school, then left when the Umbrella Corporation made him an offer he couldn't refuse. Yeah, the USAF was better than the streets of East Texas where he'd grown up, but Umbrella was better than the USAF. Better pay, better hours, less chance of getting shot.

Until today, anyhow.

He had been relaxing in a cabin in the woods when an SUV pulled up containing two of Umbrella's drones in suits. They took him to a clearing where a helicopter was waiting.

All they'd told him was that he needed to scramble his team.

"I'm on vacation," he had said. "Let One's team handle it."

"One's team is out of play," the suit had said.

"What about Ward?" he had asked, referring to the other of the three team leaders.

"Out of play also."

Carlos's eyes had widened in shock at the euphemism. Of all the commando teams employed by Security Division, One had the best of the best—it was the main reason he was able to get away with calling himself by some dopey code name—and Ward was an ex-Marine who could handle pretty much anything. If whatever they were dealing with could take out One and Ward—not to mention the likes of Melendez, Hawkins, Schlesinger, Osborne, and the other members of their respective teams—it wasn't something Carlos was overeager to face.

Not that he had a choice.

Now he sat in one of several Darkwing helicopters flying over a Raccoon City that had gone to hell in several dozen handbaskets. Apparently, something that had escaped in the Hive was now loose in the city: a virus that was the central component of Umbrella's new miracle wrinkle cream was killing people, but keeping their corpses animated and mindlessly searching for food.

When Carlos was a kid, his family had moved around a lot as *papí* tried to get work. For a while, they lived in Lubbock, and there was this beaten-down old movie house that only showed monster movies. Carlos and Jorge, his current best friend—each new home brought a new best friend, since the old ones had fathers who were actually capable of keeping jobs and generally staying on the right side of the law—spent many a night watching Frankenstein's monster, werewolves, mummies, mutated insects, space aliens, vampires, and every other creature that wanted to destroy humanity.

Including zombies.

The last night he was in Lubbock, before Carlos, *mamí, papí,* and his older sister, Consuela, packed up and headed for San Antonio, Carlos and Jorge saw a double feature: *Abbott and Costello Meet the Mummy* and *Dawn of the Dead.* He still remembered that night with perfect clarity, especially the argument afterward, since it was the last time Carlos and Jorge would ever speak to each other.

Carlos had always been partial to mummies—still was, in fact; he loved the two recent mummy pictures, especially the cool guy with the long hair and the beard—but Jorge thought the zombies were scarier.

Looking down from his vantage point in the Darkwing at the shambling things trudging through the Raccoon City streets that looked completely human and yet didn't look human in the least, Carlos decided that Jorge was right.

He turned his gaze back to his team. Nicholai Sokolov, his second-in-command, sat across from him, a grim look on his face.

The rest of the team sat on the facing benches of the Darkwing, all wearing ear- and mouthpieces that allowed them to talk to each other over the noise of the rotors. J.P.

KEITH R.A. DeCANDIDO

Askegren, the ex-cop from Virginia who always had a toothpick in the side of his mouth. Jack Carter and Sam O'Neill, who were, like Carlos, recruited out of the USAF, but had quit to join Umbrella so they could start dating each other. Yuri Loginov, Nicholai's fellow Russian, a former KGB operative in the days before the Soviet Union's fall. And their medic, Jessica Halprin, who'd retired from the Navy Medical Corps and joined Umbrella.

They looked ready for anything.

Carlos wondered how they could truly be ready for this, though.

Their jackass of a supervisor, Major Able Cain, had briefed them before sending them out. The upshot was that they needed to contain the damage. If anyone showed the signs of infection, they were to be contained. If they showed that they had succumbed, the only way to stop them was cranial or spinal trauma.

If Cain had any concern about the sheer volume of human lives being sacrificed to Umbrella's incompetence—because nothing short of total incompetence could explain a disaster like this—he didn't show it, the heartless SOB.

Then again, if it had been Cain who'd recruited Carlos out of air force instead of the corporate flunky who had approached him all those years ago, Carlos probably would've turned down Umbrella's offer. People like Cain made Carlos ill. In fact, it was the presence of people like Cain that made Carlos want to leave the armed forces for what he thought was the less cutthroat world of corporate security.

It seemed he'd miscalculated on several fronts.

Carlos turned back to the open door on the side of the Darkwing, which was now looking down at an office building roof.

The roof had a small stairwell access, and that door was open. Carlos saw two people, a man and a woman, rushing toward the door from the stairwell.

When the man made it through the doorway, he slammed the door shut behind him.

The man clambered over the far rooftop cornice out of sight. Perhaps there was a fire escape down there he could use—or maybe he just planned to climb down the façade.

Then the door burst open, and the woman ran out, quickly followed by a sea of zombies.

One of the things that had concerned Carlos in the briefing was whether he'd be able to tell someone who was alive from someone who was undead.

He no longer had that concern. Even from this distance, it was fairly obvious that the woman was very much alive and her pursuers were very much not.

Putting his hand to his ear, Carlos said to the pilot, "Lipinski, take us down!"

Lipinski's voice sounded in Carlos's earpiece. "I can't."

Carlos wasn't about to put up with this. "Take us *down!*"

"Wind shear's too strong! I'd lose the chopper!"

"Goddammit." He was not about to let that woman die.

Carlos reached under the bench and pulled out a high-tensile cable. He clipped one end to his belt, and handed the rest of it to his second-in-command. Nicholai still had a grim look on his face.

Of course, the big man *always* had a grim look on his face when they were on duty. Carlos knew it was an affectation. For whatever reason, Nicholai was determined to live up to the stereotype of the pessimistic Russian. He even retained his thick accent, even though he and his family had emigrated to the United States when he was three.

It certainly had an effect on the people under his command. They responded to him, his accent, bearing, and size making him more fearsome than even Carlos—no slouch himself at intimidation when he put his mind to it.

But Carlos had also seen Nicholai's true colors, which usually came out after you got a vodka or six in him. Then his shirt became untucked—in fact, you could measure how many vodkas he'd had by how far his shirt had come out of his pants—his accent wavered, and he smiled. Sometimes he even laughed.

"Tie me off, Nicholai."

Nicholai certainly wasn't laughing now. "What?"

Carlos didn't bother to answer. He just unholstered his twin Colt .45s and leapt out the side door toward the roof.

He was not going to let that woman die.

Nicholai's booming voice sounded both in his earpiece and over the noise of the Darkwing's rotors. "Carlos! Jesus Christ!"

The wind pounded into Carlos's face, the roof getting closer and closer. For a second, he was worried that Nicholai wouldn't actually tie him off.

Then he heard the cursing in his earpiece—it was in Russian, and the only distinct word Carlos picked out was *"chyort"*—and he knew all was well.

Before the line even went taut, Carlos started shooting. The Colts kicked against his wrists with each shot, but the bullets found their marks, taking down one zombie after another.

The line went taut about six feet above the roof. It felt like someone had gut-punched Carlos, but he ignored it. Pausing just long enough to hit the quick-release on his belt, Carlos fell the rest of the way to the roof, landing squarely on his feet.

Ignoring the shooting pains that his landing briefly sent up his calves, he recommenced shooting, the reports of the Colts drowning out the Darkwing's rotors and the litany of Russian profanity in his earpiece.

Both Colts clicked empty at the same time. At that point, the only people left standing on the roof were Carlos, the woman he was trying to rescue—

—and one zombie.

When his family lived in Dallas, Carlos had taken a martial arts class. He never got to finish it, but one thing he'd mastered in nothing flat was the spinning heel-kick. After seeing someone do one in one of the old movies he and Jorge saw in Lubbock, he was determined to learn how to do it himself. So in the class it was the first thing he learned, and he got real good at it before *papí*'s latest screwup necessitated a move to Austin.

One of those spin-kicks took down the zombie, snapping its neck with a satisfying crack.

In his earpiece, he heard Nicholai scrambling the rest of the team. They'd be down with him on the roof in a minute.

He turned to see if the woman was okay. She was cradling one arm with the other one and standing perilously close to the edge of the roof—not far from where the man who'd shut the door in her face had climbed down.

"You're okay," he said slowly. "Come away from the edge."

The wind was still pretty fierce—Carlos could see why Lipinski didn't want to land the Darkwing—and he was half-afraid that a gust would take the woman over the side.

However, the woman wouldn't budge. She turned to look down over the edge of the roof. It was at least twenty stories down—a fall would surely kill her. There were enough dead people in Raccoon City today; Carlos saw no reason to add to the tally.

"Step over to me," he said. "Everything's okay."

"No," the woman said in a hollow voice, "it's not."

She held out her arm. Carlos could see the bite marks on her forearm and wrist. He felt his stomach clench at the sight.

"I've seen what happens to you once you're bitten. There's no going back."

Behind him, Carlos could hear the rest of his team rappelling down from the Darkwing, as expected.

"We can help you." Carlos tried to sound reassuring, but he wasn't sure he could pull it off. Their mission objective was to contain anyone who was infected but not yet in the zombified state. With Cain, Carlos couldn't be a hundred percent sure that they'd be treated well, but at least they'd have a chance.

The woman shook her head and took a step backward.

Carlos found himself moving in slow motion. The woman moved so deceptively fast, just stepping backward like that, that he was caught off guard. But no matter how fast he moved, it was already too late.

He got to the edge of the roof barely a second later, but it might as well have been an hour for all the good it did. He peered over the side to see the broken, shattered body of this woman whose life he thought he'd saved.

And he didn't even know her name.

"My God."

The voice was Nicholai's. The big man was standing next to Carlos, his usually grim look replaced with one of horror. Askegren was right behind him, his toothpick falling out of his mouth as it hung open.

Carlos suspected that the same look was on his own face.

"Definitely not a good vacation," he muttered.

"What was that?" Nicholai asked.

Shaking his head, Carlos said, "Nothing. Let's get a move on."

ΠΙΠΕ

For the second time in recent memory, Alice Abernathy woke up naked.

This time, though, instead of a shower curtain, she was dressed in a flimsy hospital gown that barely covered her. Also this time, she remembered who and what she was, and what had happened to her.

Instead of a running shower, she was being pelted with something else.

No, not pelted. Attached.

Wires. They'd put wires into her. They were in her legs and her torso and her arms and her head.

She sat up.

PAIN!

Awful horrible mind-numbing excruciating searing boiling *pain* that ravaged every fiber of her being.

She ripped one of the wires out of her left arm.

The process of ripping out the wire made the pain infinitely, impossibly worse.

But then it subsided.

That emboldened her to tear out the ones in her right arm.

Same thing: worse pain at first, subsiding to something almost resembling tolerable.

She saved the two attached to the sides of her head for last.

As horrendously, wretchedly bad as the pain had been when she first woke up, the pain she felt when she tore the wires out of her head was several thousand quantum leaps worse.

By the time the white-hot agony had dimmed to a throbbing deep ache, she tried to take stock of her surroundings.

She had awakened on an examination bed with half a dozen lights shining down on it. Now, though, she was on the floor in front of it.

She couldn't make her legs move.

Looking around, she saw that each of the wires she'd rent from her flesh led to the ceiling.

Aside from the lights, the one door, the wires, and the exam table, the room was white and empty, save for a mirror.

Alice was pretty sure it was a one-way window.

Somehow, she managed to get to her feet. Her legs seemed not to remember how to function properly.

Stumbling over to the mirror/window, she slammed a fist into it. Calling for help.

If anyone heard her, they gave no indication of it.

She wondered how long she'd been unconscious on that bed.

She wondered where Matt was.

She wondered if she'd heard Cain properly, and if he was truly insane enough to reopen the Hive after so many had died down there.

Alice Abernathy remembered everything now. She remembered reading about the T-virus. She remembered thinking something needed to be done about it. She remembered meeting with Lisa Broward and arranging to give her the information about the T-virus so she could get it to people who would expose Umbrella's involvement with this despicable activity. She remembered sex with Spence, then waking up to find him gone. She remembered getting into the shower, then being hit with the nerve gas. She remembered waking up to find herself amnesiac, and accompanying One and his team of commandos, along with an equally amnesiac Spence and an RCPD cop named Matt Addison into the Hive.

She remembered the revelation that Spence was the one who'd unleashed the T-virus and that Matt wasn't a cop, but Lisa's outside contact, part of an organization dedicated to bringing Umbrella down.

She remembered watching as One and his entire team were killed: One himself, Danilova, Warner, and Vance by the security system; Kaplan and Spence by the licker; J.D. and Rain by the undead creatures that were all that remained of the Hive's employees. She remembered making her escape with Matt after killing the licker, only to be captured by Cain.

And she remembered something else, too. A memo

she'd written to Cain pointing out a design flaw in the card-swipe mechanisms that unlocked the secure doors throughout Umbrella: a well-placed sharp point could disrupt the circuits and cause the doors to open.

Cain had never acknowledged the memo. Alice was willing to bet that he hadn't bothered to fix the problem. Cain was an arrogant ass.

Alice grabbed one of the blood-soaked wires that had recently been attached to her arm. She slid it into the card-swipe mechanism, and poked around until the door unlocked.

Nope, he'd never fixed the problem.

Asshole.

She walked the hallways of what she now recognized as the Raccoon City Hospital; the wing she was in had been donated by Umbrella, and they used it for their own purposes fairly regularly.

The hallway was utterly deserted.

No doctors, no nurses, no patients.

Nothing. And no one.

The quiet was deafening. Not only was there no sign of human activity, there was no sign of the possibility of human activity.

Passing a closet, she grabbed a doctor's lab coat and put it on over the flimsy coverall.

Eventually she found the front door and walked out.

What she saw made the Hive look like a day at the park.

Abandoned, smashed vehicles: buses, cars, bicycles, motorcycles, news vans.

Broken pavement, overturned garbage cans, damaged buildings, broken glass, cracked façades, garbage strewn about, streetlamps knocked over, smoke, bonfires.

Blood *everywhere*.

But no bodies.

Slowly, walking gingerly on bare feet, trying to avoid the worst of the shattered pavement, rocks, and broken glass, she proceeded down the street.

A nearby newsstand displayed several copies of the late-afternoon edition of the *Raccoon City Times*. The front-page headline read THE DEAD WALK!

The fuckers had reopened the Hive and let the infected workers loose.

Assholes.

Still, Alice saw no people—living or dead.

Or undead.

She knew, however, that that wouldn't last.

Two of the dozens of abandoned, shattered vehicles near her were RCPD patrol cars. She checked in one, then the other—the second gave her what she wanted.

A shotgun.

She checked to see that it was fully loaded.

It was.

Alice pumped the shotgun.

TEN

"It was the best of times, it was the worst of times," Jill Valentine muttered to herself as she abandoned her car.

Her quoting Dickens to herself was prompted by the tale of two cities she had witnessed on her drive from the station house to the Ravens' Gate Bridge—or, rather, the approach to the bridge.

Parts of Raccoon City were still full of people, many of them trying to leave, or fending off zombie attacks.

Parts of Raccoon City were a total ghost town of abandoned cars, abandoned buildings, and significant collateral damage to both. She had barely been able to navigate the Porsche through some of it. For the first time, she wished she had gotten herself an SUV. But only idiots drove off-road vehicles in the city.

Of course, the world, as she well knew, was overstocked with idiots.

The main approach to the bridge was a tangle of abandoned cars. There was no way Jill was going to get through.

Luckily, she had no reason not to abandon the car. Nice as the Porsche was, it was just a thing. The same uncle who'd left her the brownstone and the Porsche had also left her enough in her bank account that she could buy new things.

The only items that mattered to her were the twin automatics in her shoulder and thigh holsters, the pack of cigarettes in her pocket that she'd retrieved from the Porsche's glove compartment, and the cards in her wallet that provided access to her money. Everything else— her clothes, her awards, her pool table, her CDs, and, yes, her badge—was eminently replaceable.

While the Raccoon side of the bridge was clogged with abandoned vehicles—including, to Jill's bitter amusement, dozens of SUVs—the Ravens' Gate side was equally clogged with people, all of whom were trying to get out of the city.

The answer to Jill's immediate query as to what was slowing them down so much was answered when she got a good look at the terminus of the Ravens' Gate side. A large wall had been constructed on the other side, covered in razor wire and staffed by people in Hazmat suits and people carrying very large guns. The only way through the wall, which looked to be made of concrete, was through a narrow gate at the bridge road.

To Jill's great annoyance, the wall, the people in the Hazmat suits, and the people with the guns all were emblazoned with the Umbrella Corporation logo.

Naturally.

No, wait, not all of them. As she pushed her way forward, she saw a few RCPD uniforms helping out. But it was obvious that their work was solely supportive.

Umbrella was running the show.

Why even bother having a police force? Or a government? Let the Corporation run everything for us!

If Jill's experiences following Arklay hadn't numbed her, she would have felt the urge to throw up at this crass abuse of power.

But for now, she just wanted to get the hell out of Dodge. In retrospect, she should have left Raccoon as soon as they suspended her. After all, a cop couldn't survive if she couldn't rely on her fellow cops.

Henderson and the rest of the RCPD brass hadn't backed her up—they'd fed her to the wolves dressed in the snappy suits favored by the Umbrella Corporation.

She owed them nothing. So she was leaving.

All she had to do was plow through the crowd.

A medical station had been set up where a doctor was checking people over as they approached the gate, guarded by Umbrella's thugs—

—and one man dressed in a S.T.A.R.S. uniform.

"Peyton!" she screamed, but she couldn't be heard over the din of the people impatiently waiting for their turns to be examined so they could leave.

As she pushed her way through the crowd toward the gate, she noticed the doctor performing the examinations. White male, late twenties, but with a look on his face that Jill knew all too well—mostly from homicide cops in the third day of a red-ball case, on their sixth straight shift with no sleep, surviving only on coffee, cigarettes, and the tattered remains of their fortitude. This doc looked like he was ready to fall over, but he soldiered on.

Jill admired his dedication. If only she shared it.

Right now, the doc was checking over a man, woman, and child, presumably a family. "They're clean," Jill heard him say in a haggard voice that bespoke a man three times his age, "let them pass."

Two of the Umbrella thugs escorted the threesome to the gate.

"Next!" the doc said.

A tide of humanity surged forward, barely kept in check by the thugs and cops. Jill let herself be carried along by that wave, bringing her closer to her boss.

Peyton Wells was Jill's immediate supervisor and, unlike *his* immediate supervisor, that scum-sucking weasel Henderson, he had stuck up for Jill after the Arklay incident. "Jill Valentine don't make shit up," was his exact phrasing in his statement on the incident. He had always stood by his people, and his people always stood by him. You needed that kind of loyalty to survive in a high-pressure squad like S.T.A.R.S.

That was why the brass's utter disregard—or maybe lack of understanding—of that loyalty hurt Jill so much.

"Peyton!" she cried again, now that she was closer, even as the guards let an old man and a teenage girl through.

This time, Peyton heard her. Up until then, he'd had his usual hard-ass expression on, but at the sight of her, he actually looked relieved. "Valentine!" He pointed at her while looking at one of the Umbrella thugs. "Let her through, she's RCPD—one of my S.T.A.R.S. people."

The Umbrella thug frowned. "She's not in uniform."

Peyton rolled his eyes. "Right, 'cause when *I'm* off duty and I see walking dead people tearing up the town, first thing *I'm* gonna do is worry about my wardrobe. Will you let her through, please?"

Jill smiled as the thugs cleared a path for her to join Peyton.

"Glad you're here," he said. "We could use a hand."

She refrained from saying that she wasn't glad to be there and had no interest in lending a hand. Peyton deserved better.

But before she could say anything, the old man the doc was looking at keeled over.

"Oh, my God," the teenager wailed, "Daddy!"

While the guards and the doc all stood around, the girl knelt down and started loosening his shirt.

How pathetic was it, Jill thought, that this little girl had more common sense than the so-called trained professionals?

"He's not breathing! It's his heart—he has a weak heart."

That, to Jill, explained some of her swift reaction—she'd possibly been through this kind of thing before.

However, as soon as she began applying mouth-to-mouth, the doc went into a panic. "Get away from him!"

Ignoring the doc, the girl kept up with the entire CPR routine—mouth-to-mouth, massaging the heart, the whole bit.

The doc looked at Peyton. "Get her away from him."

Letting out a grunt of annoyance, Peyton nonetheless reached down and pulled the girl off her father.

Jill was disgusted. That girl was trying to save her father's life, and *this* was how she was treated? Jill needed to get out of this dump, *now*.

The girl struggled in Peyton's muscular arms. "No, let me go, I've got to—"

Suddenly, the old man's eyes popped open.

When he'd walked up to the gate, the man's eyes had been brown.

Now they were milky white.

Oh, shit.

Moving with a speed Jill wouldn't have credited so old a man with having, he bit Peyton right on the leg.

"Aaaaahhhhhh!"

This did nothing to calm the crowd. Already surging against the barely adequate barricade of guards, they went into a total frenzy at the sight of Peyton being bitten.

Jill took out her automatic and put a bullet in the old man's head.

The teenager screamed. "Noooooo! Daddy! *Daddy!* You *killed* him!"

"He was already dead," Jill said.

The girl ran off, knocking down one of the Umbrella thugs. Another thug stepped into his spot to keep the crowd in check, but this mess was only going to get worse.

Jill noticed that, as the thug went down, his headset had fallen off. She reached down to pick it up and was about to give it to the thug, who was shaking his head in an attempt to clear it, when she heard voices over the earpiece.

A young voice: *"Sir?"*

The next voice spoke with a German accent: *"It's here. It's reached the gate."*

A third voice, sounding officious: *"All right, then. We don't have a choice. We have to keep it contained."*

German: *"Close them."*

Young guy: *"Sir?"*

German: *"Seal the gates."*

Young guy: *"But our men are still out there!"*

German: *"Just do it."*

Jill looked up at the wall. The gate started to swing shut.

"Shit, this hurts."

Turning around, Jill saw that no one had bothered to bind Peyton's wound. In fact, the doc was suddenly nowhere to be found.

That just figured.

There was an abandoned first-aid kit, which Jill snagged. She quickly bound Peyton's wound. That the old man had even been able to bite through Peyton's pants and break the skin was pretty impressive.

As she tied off the bandage, Jill said, "Dammit, Peyton, you should've got out while you had the chance."

"These are our people, Jill."

Jill snorted and shook her head. Loyal to the end. Him and Quinn both. They'd probably both get posthumous medals.

Fat lotta good it would do them.

"Out of my way! I'm a celebrity, goddammit!"

Amazingly enough, this worked, as a sea of panicky Raccoon City citizens actually parted to let a perky-looking woman through. Jill recognized her as a reporter from one of the TV stations, but she couldn't remember which one. Tammy Morehead? Theresa Morehouse? Something like that.

Then a voice boomed out overhead. Jill looked up to see one of the Umbrella goons standing on the wall holding a megaphone.

"This is a biohazard quarantine area."

The voice belonged to the German guy.

"What's going on here?" the reporter lady screamed up at the wall.

Ignoring her—or maybe he couldn't hear her—the German repeated his words: *"This is a biohazard quarantine area. Due to risk of infection, you cannot be allowed to leave the city."*

"What are you talking about?" the reporter demanded.

Jill almost screamed that he couldn't hear her, but decided she wasn't worth the effort.

"All appropriate measures are being taken. The situation is under control. Please return to your homes."

If it wasn't so colossally stupid, Jill would have

laughed. She almost did anyhow, as laughter was the only alternative to eating her gun.

Return to their homes. Right. Raccoon City was a cemetery, with new graves being dug every second. By closing that gate, this German fuckhead had just sentenced them all to death.

What was worse, Jill suspected that the German knew it. And didn't care.

Typical Umbrella.

The citizenry was, understandably, a bit put off by these instructions.

"Return to our homes?"

"Are you insane?"

"What homes?"

"Let us through!"

The people started surging forward. The thugs and cops were having an increasingly harder time subduing them, as desperation lent strength to their actions.

Or maybe the predicament was weakening the thugs and cops as well, Jill thought. After all, they were just as trapped as the rest of them.

This is a biohazard quarantine area. Please return to your homes.

Jill wondered if the German had a pull-string in the back that let him just repeat that phrase over and over.

She looked at Peyton, still trying to hold people back and keep them calm, even with his wounded leg.

She thought about Quinn, staying behind at his desk.

"These are our people, Jill."

"My shift ain't over yet."

Fuck.

She yelled up at the wall, "There are injured people here! They need medical attention!"

In response, the German put down his megaphone and raised an automatic weapon—an MP5K, from the look of it.

He fired a dozen rounds into the air.

All noise and movement stopped.

Raising the megaphone again, the German said, *"You have fifteen seconds to turn around and return to the city."*

Six more thugs took up positions on the wall around the German. Jill wondered which was the young guy she'd overheard on the headset. They also had MP5Ks.

The German handed the megaphone to the man next to him, who spoke into it.

"Use of live ammunition has been authorized."

Yup—it was the guy on the headset.

"He can't shoot people!" the reporter woman said.

Terri Morales, *that* was her name. Jill had talked to her several times back when she was a reporter, before she screwed up an exposé of Councilman Miller. After that, they put her on weather—which was better than she deserved. Anybody who could screw up an exposé of *that* bastard didn't deserve to be in a news reporting position.

As for what she had said, Jill wasn't worried. These were corporate thugs. Corporations were cruel, yes, sometimes vicious, often uncaring. But they were never sadistic.

"Fifteen . . . fourteen . . . thirteen . . . twelve . . ."

The German nodded at the thugs on the wall. They all raised their rifles.

"Eleven . . . ten . . ."

Peyton looked at Jill. "He's not bluffing."

"Nine . . . eight . . ."

Jill couldn't believe it. "They won't fire into a crowd."

"Seven . . . six . . ."

"Get them back."

For whatever reason, Peyton Wells was sure that they were going to fire into the crowd.

Peyton had trusted Jill's judgment when nobody else did. She could do no less now.

"Five . . . four . . ."

Besides, if the German would authorize closing the gates, why *not* fire into a crowd of innocent people? They were already dead anyhow.

"Move!" Jill screamed. "Get away from the wall!"

Peyton did likewise, as did the other RCPD cops.

"Three . . . two . . ."

After a moment, so did the Umbrella thugs. They tried to force the people back, make them move away from the wall.

"One . . ."

The next thing Jill heard were multiple reports of assault rifles being shot straight downward from the top of the wall.

ELEVEΠ

If Timothy Cain heard the screams of the people he had just ordered shot, he didn't show it as he descended the metal staircase that took him and Giddings down to the base camp.

Instead, he spoke into his headset.

"Ravens' Gate is secure, but I just lost contact with squads one and two within the city. Squads three through seven are in full retreat."

"Is there any chance of containment?"

"No, sir. Suppression measures have failed. We can't contain it. The infection's spreading faster than anyone could have anticipated."

"That's for damn sure." The man on the other end sighed audibly. *"All right, we'll have to activate Nemesis, per your recommendation. Out."*

Cain nodded and turned to Giddings. They were now approaching one of the several dozen inflatable workshops that had been hastily constructed once this base perimeter had been set up. Each had the distinctive U of the corporation logo emblazoned on the side.

From his Gulf days, Cain remembered several ops that had been perfectly planned and competently executed, yet still failed because of something that had happened in the desert. The desert was, literally, a force of nature, and men's plans couldn't always succeed under those circumstances.

Back when he was a green private, his first lieutenant had always said, "Some days, the desert wins."

Today, the desert was winning.

The op had gone down as planned, but the T-virus was just out of control.

To Giddings, he said, "Prep the C89 and get it in the air. Activation of the Nemesis Program has been confirmed."

Giddings nodded and moved off. Cain headed toward the copter pad, only to see the wheelchair-bound form of Dr. Charles Ashford.

Ashford was one of the primary reasons why Cain took home such a large paycheck. Many of Umbrella's most lucrative—and top-secret—contracts were linked to Ashford's brilliant viral work.

So, of course, was today's disaster.

But Ashford was also to be treated pretty much like royalty. Cain's bosses had made it quite clear to him that Ashford was more important than *anyone* in or around

Raccoon City, including Cain himself. That was why he, along with Umbrella's other top scientists, had been evac-ed this morning. Shortly before closing the gate, Cain had been ordered to have them all taken to a secure location several dozen miles from here. Raccoon wasn't safe, and these were resources that needed protecting.

Right now, the scientist was regarding Cain with an annoyed expression.

"Dr. Ashford."

"What was all the shooting?"

"Nothing the Science Division need concern itself about. Shouldn't you be on the chopper?"

"I'm not going."

Cain tried not to let his own annoyance show. This, he didn't need. He looked over at the SUVs parked nearby—one of which was conspicuous by its absence.

"Doctor, I was instructed to get you and the other scientists out of the hot zone. You're too important to Umbrella to be put at risk."

"I'm not leaving, not till I have my daughter."

So there it was. As Cain had suspected when Stein and whichever of the Friedberger brothers—Cain could never keep them straight—had failed to arrive with Angie Ashford, the crippled man's daughter was still inside Raccoon City.

Which meant she was dead.

But try explaining that to a father.

"I'm sorry, truly, but the city is sealed. Even if she is still alive, I couldn't let her out. Not now—the risk of infection is too great. You must understand."

"I don't understand how any of this has happened. How could there be an outbreak?"

Cain shook his head. "I don't know."

That much was the truth. The only things they'd been able to determine for sure were when the T-virus was released into the Hive, and that Alice Abernathy was in the mansion taking a shower when it happened. They only knew that much because the mansion security cameras had managed to escape the catastrophic damage to the Red Queen, and so were recoverable.

All Abernathy's innocence did was raise more questions.

Cain looked over to see that everyone had boarded the chopper except for Ashford.

"There's really nothing you can do here, Doctor."

"I'm staying."

An urge to simply pick Ashford up and put him on the chopper nearly overwhelmed Cain, but he suppressed it. If he did that, and Ashford reported back that it had happened—which he most assuredly would—Cain's job wouldn't be worth a plugged nickel.

If Ashford wanted to stay, he was going to stay. But Cain wasn't about to let him run loose.

He signaled the chopper pilot to take off, then called Giddings over.

"Yes, sir?"

"Take Dr. Ashford to Work Area D." That was one of the tents. It included a work space, an Umbrella computer that was hooked up to the company satellite, a bunk, and a bookshelf. It would allow the doctor to keep himself busy, maybe even get some work done, while futilely waiting for his daughter to return to him. "Keep him secure there."

"Yes, sir."

Giddings moved behind Ashford and wheeled his chair into the tent in question. Moments later, he came back out, sealed the tent, then called over one of the commandos, a recent recruit named Noyce.

"Watch him," Giddings said. "He's not to leave."

"Sir," Noyce said smartly.

Cain nodded in affirmation.

Then he moved to the command center they'd set up behind the copter pad. They were missing plenty of people in Raccoon City; after losing One and his team, Ward and his team, and about five hundred employees, compounding it with two squads going missing was starting to get irritating.

It was going to cost Umbrella some serious money to cover this up.

†WELVE

The city looked different to Alice Abernathy—beyond the obvious.

Colors were sharper. Details were easier to make out. Shapes were more distinct.

And she could see farther than before, as well.

The bastards had done something to her.

Sometime between when they gave her the sedative at the mansion and when she woke up in the hospital, they had done something to her.

She didn't know what, but it had changed her.

Knowing Umbrella, it couldn't be anything good.

As she walked the streets, she saw very few people. Some were alive—easy to pick out, they were the ones who were screaming and scared out of their minds— some were walking corpses.

Sometimes she saw one type grappling with the other. If they were at close quarters, Alice would yell at the living one to break the dead one's neck or, if armed, to aim for the head.

If they weren't at close quarters, Alice just took the shotgun she'd liberated from the RCPD cruiser and blew the dead one's head off.

The living ones rarely were grateful. They usually just ran like hell.

Alice couldn't blame them. A woman in a hospital gown carrying a shotgun wasn't exactly someone you wanted to hang around and have a chat with.

Walking the broken streets of Raccoon City, she found herself disgusted with the very concept of greed.

Greed had created this nightmare:

Umbrella's greed in creating the T-virus in the first place, as the basis for a wrinkle cream used to feed the egos of vain fools, and perhaps also as something to sell to the highest bidder as a bioterror weapon.

And Spence Parks's greed leading him to steal the virus and its antigen so he could sell it to his own highest bidder, and to infect the entire Hive and condemn five hundred people to death in order to cover his tracks.

Looking back, Alice should have seen it coming. Spence had made no bones about his greed from the moment they met, and were partnered as the faux married couple assigned to guard the mansion. He said he had abandoned his job at the Chicago Police Department without a moment's thought because of the paycheck that came with working for Umbrella's Security Division.

But Alice had never paid close attention to him beyond how good he was in the bed they shared and how well he did his job as her partner. Even though her training, her instincts, her job description all required her to look beneath the surface.

What was it she'd said not long ago? *"Don't judge a book by its cover. First rule of Security Division."*

Alice's instincts had served her well in so many other ways, but they'd failed her with Spence.

Now Spence was dead, the Hive employees were all dead, Rain and the rest of One's team were dead, half of Raccoon City was dead with the other half likely to follow suit, she had no idea what had happened to Matt—and it was all because of greed.

That, and stupidity. She knew Cain, and this had his fingerprints all over it. For all that asshole talked about efficiency, his operations were always sloppy and reckless. He never took collateral damage into account, and all too often wound up living out the worst-case scenario of his contingencies.

That was certainly the case here.

The last thing Alice had heard Cain say in the mansion was that he was reopening the Hive, which was quite possibly the stupidest thing anyone could have done under those circumstances.

Alice had thought herself to be wandering aimlessly through downtown Raccoon, but as soon as she turned the corner onto an out-of-the-way street, she knew she had a particular destination in mind, if only subconsciously.

She walked up to a building with a ten-step stoop that led to a single entryway with three doors. Two led to storefronts that took up the ground floor—a newsstand and a flooring place. The third led to an apartment-building lobby. Adjacent to the stoop was another staircase, which led down to a door with a modest sign emblazoned with the words **CHE BUONO.**

The last time Alice had been in Raccoon proper was when she had taken Lisa Broward to lunch. Alice had discovered that Lisa, the person in charge of maintaining security on the massive Red Queen computer network, had a personal vendetta against Umbrella relating to the death of a former coworker of hers. So Alice had recruited her to help expose Umbrella's development of the T-virus, which was in violation of national law, international law, and any number of treaties the United States had signed over the years.

Unbeknownst to Alice at the time, Lisa had been planted in Umbrella by her brother, Matt Addison, who was part of a secret group dedicated to exposing Umbrella for the shits they were.

Spence's greed had managed to muck that up, too. Lisa had been all set to deliver the T-virus to Matt, who was meeting her at the mansion. Instead, Matt found himself caught up in the nightmare Spence had caused.

Alice had first found Che Buono one Valentine's Day. She was wandering around downtown feeling sorry for herself because she was alone on this day that celebrated couplehood. Che Buono—an Italian restaurant run by a small family named Figlia who'd emigrated from Italy in order to open a restaurant in America—was the only place that had a free table, and Alice had the best meal of her life there.

She proceeded gingerly down the stairs to see if the Figlias were all right.

Inside was a disaster. The six tables were all overturned, the chairs strewn about, many of them broken. The photographs of Italy on the wall were askew, knocked down, many of them damaged. Worst of all, the painting of the Ponte Vecchio in Florence that was the restaurant's centerpiece was covered in blood.

Alice saw no bodies. She wondered if that was a good sign or a bad one.

Then she heard a noise.

The kitchen door opened and four people came shuffling out.

Anna Figlia, the old woman who served as the restaurant's maître d'.

Her son, Luigi, and his wife, Antonia, who did all the cooking.

Luigi and Antonia's teenage daughter, Rosa, who was the main server.

As one, they moved toward Alice, their eyes milky, their mouths hinged open exposing black teeth that seemed almost to be aimed at Alice's neck.

Once, the sight of these four faces had been a refuge. Coming to Che Buono had been a safe haven from the growing frustration with working for despicable people who asked her to do despicable things for despicable causes. She had deliberately brought Lisa here because

KEiTH R.A. DeCanDiDO

she knew it would bring out the best in her, and show Alice if she was truly to be trusted. She cherished the memory of the look on Lisa's face when she first tasted the veal parmigiano, claiming it was the finest she'd had since she was a kid eating in one of the many Italian places she and her family had gone to in New York City.

Tears welling in her eyes, Alice raised her shotgun and squeezed the trigger four times.

Then she turned and left Che Buono for the last time.

She bumped against the door frame as she exited. A sliver of pain shot through her forearm, and she realized that she'd cut it.

Ignoring the wound, she moved on through the streets.

One storefront eventually caught her eye: **SURPLUS AND MORE.** It was a good old-fashioned army/navy surplus store—just the place to go for one-stop postapocalyptic shopping.

If nothing else, she was almost out of shotgun ammo.

As she moved through the store, mentally calculating what she'd realistically need versus what she could easily carry, she suddenly convulsed. A spasm of pain swept through her entire body.

Her arms felt especially strange, and she looked at them only to see a peculiar rippling effect—like there was something moving under her skin.

With horror, she remembered where she'd seen such an effect before: on Matt Addison's wounded arm, right before they were taken by Cain and his goons at the mansion.

Then she noticed something else: the cut on her arm had completely healed.

Another wave of pain slammed into her, and she almost stumbled to the floor. This was worse than the pain she'd suffered when she woke up in the hospital, worse even than when she'd pulled the leads out of her flesh.

God, what was *happening* to her?

The pain started to subside. She looked around the store for a mirror, found one, and ran toward it.

Her eyes widened in shock.

The patches of hair that had been shaved off to allow the leads to be placed on her head had grown back in, the wounds from those leads also healed.

She looked down at her feet. Since leaving the hospital, she'd been walking barefoot on broken glass and shattered pavement, yet there wasn't a cut or bruise on her soles.

The bastards had most definitely done something to her.

Then she heard a noise.

Raising her shotgun, she turned around to find a gaggle of zombies shuffling toward her through the front door.

But before they got too close, they stopped.

Stared at her with their watery eyes.

Alice had her shotgun aimed right at the lead zombie's forehead, ready to shoot if she or any of the others attacked.

But she didn't.

Neither did the others.

They just shuffled right by her, ignoring her.

That didn't make any sense.

Oh, yeah, the bastards had done *something* to her. The question was, what?

Then she heard another noise—the revving engine of a motorcycle.

She turned and looked out the front. A Harley was headed straight for the store window.

And was *not* slowing down.

Even as she dived for cover behind the cashier's desk, the motorcycle smashed through the window with a crash that Alice found unusually loud—in part because it had been so quiet, but also, she now realized, because her hearing was, like everything else, *much* more acute now.

She stood up to see that the bike had come to a halt by crashing into a clothes rack full of fatigues. A large man in a leather jacket was slumped over the handlebars, head obscured by a pile of green camos.

As soon as she got close, the biker shot upright. She couldn't see his eyes behind the mirrored shades, but the way his mouth almost fell open was unmistakable.

Alice calmly grabbed his head, one hand on either side, and twisted.

Then she threw the biker to the ground headfirst, causing him to tumble off the bike. She located the ignition, turned it off, then wheeled the bike out of the clothes rack, standing it up against the cashier's desk.

Now she had a more efficient way of getting around town.

Even as the zombie brigade shuffled around her, ignoring her completely, Alice continued her shopping expedition, the list of what she could carry having just increased slightly.

THIRTEEN

If you'd asked Jill Valentine how she managed to escape the chaos of Ravens' Gate Bridge, she couldn't have told you.

One minute, she was screaming at everyone to get back. The next moment, gunfire. The moment after that, a sea of humanity running every which way.

Next thing she knew, she was running down the streets of Raccoon City, supporting the wounded Peyton Wells and accompanied by, of all people, Terri Morales.

Had the situation been slightly different—say, Morales wounded and Peyton in good shape—Jill would not have allowed herself to be slowed down by a wounded person. But she wasn't about to abandon Peyton.

Once those who'd survived Umbrella's skeet shoot

at Ravens' Gate managed to get to the Raccoon side of the bridge, they scattered to the four winds. Jill chose the direction the three of them went as much for its comparative emptiness as anything else. She figured the zombies would tend toward greater concentrations of people, so while most headed down Route 22 or Western Boulevard, Jill and Peyton—and Morales, who was now clinging to them like a leech—went down the less-traveled Dilmore Place, which led to a run-down residential area.

As they moved farther down Dilmore, Jill glanced over at Peyton, hobbling along with his left arm wrapped around her neck. He was getting pale and sweaty, though the latter could have been due to the heat, which hadn't abated with the sun going down.

Most of the streetlights weren't working, but plenty of bonfires and burning cars lit their way. Jill caught sight of a large church at the end of the road where Dilmore met Lyons Street.

What better place to seek sanctuary?

She tried to reassure Peyton. "We'll rest up soon."

"Don't worry about me," he said, trying desperately to sound tough and failing miserably.

That more than anything showed how sick Peyton was. He usually had no trouble sounding tough.

Morales, who had been mercifully quiet up until then, suddenly burst into a torrent of words.

"What the *fuck* is going on!? They were shooting at people! *Innocent* people! Why didn't you do something, you're the police!"

The ex-reporter did have a point. After all, it wasn't like Umbrella had any standing as a law-enforcement or military agency. The words of that guy on the wall notwithstanding, they couldn't "authorize" use of live ammunition anywhere outside a firing range.

But ultimately, the only person with true authority was the one holding the biggest gun. Right now, that was Umbrella.

However, Jill had neither the interest nor the patience to explain it to Raccoon 7's weather girl.

When they reached the church gate, Jill said, "Inside. Let's get under cover."

The church was a huge Gothic structure that looked like something Tim Burton had asked Frank Lloyd Wright to build when both of them were drunk. The funky architecture and giant gargoyles were spooky enough in the firelit darkness outside, but apparently the electricity wasn't on full bore inside, either. The roof was high in here, the shadows long, the light sources few and far between. Over the front door was a huge stained-glass window depicting Lucifer being cast out of heaven and into hell—which Jill recognized more from reading *Paradise Lost* in college than from any religious training. A huge cross hung above the altar.

Just as Jill was starting to wonder if this was such a hot idea, a voice sounded from one of the many shadows.

"That's it! No closer!"

A figure stepped out. It was a disheveled white man, probably early thirties, holding a .357 Magnum that looked about as comfortable in his hand as it would've looked in Morales's.

Jill had seen the expression on the man's face dozens of times over the years since she'd joined S.T.A.R.S., usually in hostage takers and kidnappers: the uniquely crazed look of someone who had nothing to lose and carried a high-caliber weapon.

Putting on her best negotiator voice—and wishing that Goldblume, their actual negotiator, were here—Jill said, "It's okay. We're not those things."

"This is my place! I found it! I'm hiding here!"

Morales butted in drily. "I think it's big enough for all of us."

The man started waving the .357. "You'll lead them here! You have to get out!"

To Jill's shock, Morales got right in the man's face. She either had balls of steel or was dumb as a post. Or both.

Jill's money was on both.

"We're not going back outside! You got it?"

The man put the .357's muzzle right at Morales's face. "Don't tell me—"

"Okay, *just cool it!* Put the gun down!"

Both of them backed off at Peyton's command, which echoed off the high ceilings.

Jill smiled. Apparently Peyton *could* still sound tough.

The man lowered the gun.

Walking up to him and holding out a hand, Jill said, "You might want to give that to me."

"I don't think so." The man was still shaken, but he sounded a bit less crazy.

Peyton looked at Morales. "And you—take it easy."

Jill did likewise. "Plenty of ways to get killed here without getting yourself shot."

Morales said nothing in reply. Instead, she looked down at her hand. Only then did Jill notice that she was holding something small and metallic. Had she given anything like a shit about Terri Morales, she might have asked what it was.

Instead, she sat in one of the pews and pulled out a cigarette. A flash of worry that she was desecrating sacred ground came over her, but it passed quickly. Zombies were roaming the streets, corporations were shooting innocent people—if there was a God, He hadn't been to Raccoon City lately.

After taking a drag, Jill noticed that Morales was now looking at her.

"Jill Valentine, right? Remember me? I covered some of your cases—before your suspension." She stuck out a hand. "Terri Morales, Raccoon 7."

Not bothering to return the offered handshake, Jill blew cigarette smoke into Morales's face. "I've seen all your work."

Morales smiled. The expression didn't really work on her face. "A fan."

"Not really. You do the weather now, right?"

The smile fell. Jill took some enjoyment from that. She indicated Peyton, who was now also seated in a pew. "Sergeant Peyton Wells."

Pointing to the item in Morales's hand, Peyton asked, "What's that you've got there?"

Morales held up the item: a small, handheld video camera. The red record light was on—Jill suspected it had been on since Morales arrived at the bridge.

"My Emmy," she said with another smile. "If any of us make it out." She pointed the camera's lens right at Peyton. "So, does the Raccoon City Police Department have a comment on what those things are?"

"The Lord's judgment."

The voice wasn't Peyton's—it echoed off the high ceilings, but Jill realized quickly that it came from the altar.

She turned to see a priest or minister or whatever he was walking toward them. His dog collar was dirty, his robes had seen better decades, and his hair looked like it hadn't been combed since the Clinton administration.

"'Behold I will bring evil upon this people, even the fruit of their thoughts, for they have not harkened unto my words, nor to my law, but rejected it.' 'Awake and sing, ye that dwell in dust, for thy dew is as the dew of herbs, and the earth shall cast out the dead.' The dead shall walk amongst the living and bring damnation unto them!"

By the time he was done, he had joined them at the front of the church.

"That's quite a speech," Jill deadpanned.

"Jeremiah," the man with the .357 muttered. "The first part, anyhow. After that was from Isaiah. Not sure about the last bit."

Morales smiled, her camera pointed right at the priest. "Yeah, that's making the final cut."

A sudden noise from behind the altar startled all of them—except the priest.

"What is that?" Peyton asked.

"It's nothing."

Jill snorted. There was no such thing as nothing in Raccoon City anymore. She made a beeline for the altar, walking around behind it to the vestry. Her eyes were starting to adjust to the dim light, but she still walked gingerly, afraid of tripping over a spare rosary or something.

No, wait, it was Catholics who used rosaries, and she didn't think this was a Catholic church. Jill had never paid attention to that stuff. Her father was a lapsed Episcopalian, her mother an unobservant Jew. If pressed, Jill would probably describe herself as an indifferent agnostic.

Today, though, she didn't know *what* to believe.

The vestry was lit by a single table lamp, which still, thanks to the smaller space, made it better lit than the main part of the church. Several tables and chairs were overturned—that seemed to be par for the course for any room in Raccoon City today.

Most notable was the streak of blood on one wall. It was consistent, her police academy-trained mind knew, with arterial spray.

Not the sort of thing you wanted to see in a priest's sanctum.

In front of her sat a woman in a chair, rocking back and forth, her head down.

"Are you all right?" Jill asked.

A voice suddenly said from behind her, "What are you doing?"

Jill nearly jumped out of her skin. Where the hell had a priest learned to sneak up on a trained S.T.A.R.S. officer like that?

Probably better to ask where a trained S.T.A.R.S. officer had learned to let her instincts dull. Answer: Raccoon City on the day the zombies took over.

"What's wrong with her?" Jill asked, suspecting the answer.

"It's my wife. She's—she's not well."

As Jill tried to move closer to the woman, the priest blocked her way.

"No!"

"Out of my way."

"She's not well, I tell you."

"Maybe I can help." Jill didn't feel too guilty about the lie. Besides, it wasn't entirely a lie. If the wife was another one of these—these creatures, shooting her in the head *would* be a help.

Pushing past the priest, she noticed that the woman was tied to the chair with electrical wire. That both verified her suspicions and explained the lack of lighting.

Then the woman looked up, and Jill saw the blood around her mouth.

"Oh, my God."

The woman started shaking back and forth in the chair, straining against her bonds.

"You're sick," Jill said to the priest.

"Just get out," he said, sounding both angry and sad.

Jill didn't know whether to feel sorry for him or shoot him.

Or both.

"Get out of my church," the priest cried. "I can help her. Exorcise this thing from her."

Jill might have believed that he was sincere—right up until she tripped and almost fell over something on the floor. Looking down, she saw a half-eaten corpse.

That explained the blood on the wall and around the woman's mouth.

She looked at the man in horror. "What have you been doing?"

"Just leave us alone!" the priest screamed.

As she watched the woman rock back and forth, back and forth, pulling with all her strength against the electrical wire, Jill realized that there was more than one way to die in this town today.

Then the woman's right hand broke free.

Jill unholstered one of her automatics.

"No!"

The priest lunged for her, spoiling her shot. But what he had in passion he lacked in strength, and it was the work of only a moment for Jill to throw him off—

—into the waiting arms of his wife.

Just as she broke free of the remaining bonds.

She caught her husband in her now-free arms, bent down, and bit him full on the neck.

The priest's screams echoed through the tiny

APOCALYPSE

vestry. Jill imagined they could be heard all the way down Dilmore.

Right up until she shot him in the head.

When he fell, she did the same to his wife.

Without a second glance, she went back out into the church.

Based on the looks on the faces of Peyton, Morales, and the man with the .357, they had indeed heard the screams.

"What happened back there?" Peyton asked.

Jill just shook her head.

108

FOURTEEN

Angus McKenzie didn't want these bloody people in his church.

All right, so technically it wasn't *his* bloody church, it was that minister's bloody church, but from the sounds of things, that wasn't an issue anymore. There'd been two gunshots, so the minister probably had one of those demons back there.

Like the demons back at the office.

He wasn't going to let them capture him. Angus McKenzie hadn't come all the way from Scotland to the United States just to be eaten alive by a demon.

All right, so telemarketing wasn't exactly the world's most glamorous profession, but it put food on the bloody table, didn't it? And he was *good* at it. The boss, he said it was the accent—that always got people interested. Made 'em think it was exotic somehow. People went for exotic, especially Americans.

Most of them by dint of having no bloody history of their own, in Angus's bloody opinion, but that was neither here nor there.

Then everyone started getting all crazy.

Angus's wife, Flora, God rest her soul, would've said that the devil had come to make them all pay for their sins. Flora was big on sins and making up for them. She'd died in great fear that she would go to hell.

As far as Angus was concerned, she had nothing to worry about. She was going to heaven, of that he had no doubt.

Angus himself was another story.

Still, nothing he'd done in his life—and he'd done plenty, he was the first to admit it—deserved being eaten alive by demons.

Not even leaving Marla to those creatures.

It had been wrong to do it, he knew that, but he couldn't help himself. When they ran up to the roof to escape the demons that their coworkers had turned into, he had to shut the roof door in her face. It was the only way he'd be safe.

Sure, it probably meant she'd die, but at least he'd live, wouldn't he?

As he climbed down from the roof, he'd heard the commotion of the demons trying to take Marla.

And he'd seen Marla fall to her death.

But it didn't matter, did it? He was alive.

He'd found a dead black git with a high-caliber gun

in his waistband. Probably some drug dealer. These blacks were always dealing drugs and killing each other. Angus thought it was a disgrace.

Less of a disgrace than condemning a coworker, an innocent girl, to die? He pushed the thought away.

He'd found sanctuary in a house of the Lord. True, it wasn't a proper Catholic church, but one of those Protestant abominations. A papist through and through, Angus normally would never have set foot in one of the heretical structures, but needs must as the devil drives.

Or, in this case, demons.

And they were bloody *everywhere*.

Here, he'd be safe.

In the arms of the Lord.

Or close to it, anyhow.

So as far as Angus McKenzie was concerned, this was *his* church.

Then that cop and the Morales girl from the telly and that girl with the two guns had showed up—then the minister. One of the bloody heathens. He was crazy, that one. From the sounds of it, the two-gun girl—she was probably a cop, too, they were always letting girls into the constabulary in this mad country—had taken care of the minister.

Now Angus had to figure out how he could get the remaining three to leave his church.

Suddenly, something moved across the ceiling. Angus looked up, but he couldn't make anything out in the bloody gloom of the place.

Damned heathens, with their nooks and crannies and inadequate light and mad architecture.

APOCALYPSE

The cop had a torch, and he flicked it on and shone it on the arched stone ceiling.

Bits of dust and plaster glowed in the torchlight.

So did the three claw marks in the stone.

Jesus bloody Christ!

"What the hell is that?"

"Over there!" the two-gun girl said, pointing toward another part of the ceiling.

Angus followed the cop's torchlight, which he shone where the woman pointed.

All it illuminated were more bloody claw marks.

"There!" Now it was the Morales girl pointing.

This time, the cop's bloody torch caught what it was moving in the shadows.

All things considered, Angus wished he hadn't bothered.

"Jesus!"

It was like something out of a nightmare.

Nominally, it had a human shape: two arms, two legs, but its spine was all bent so it could move on all fours. It looked like it had been flensed, with just corded red muscle and white bone on the surface—but it looked hard, like a rhino's leathery skin. The bloody thing's fingers and toes ended in huge claws, which explained the markings.

The head, though, was what held Angus's attention.

The squared-off mouth was bad enough—it was chock-full of jagged teeth and a massive bloody tongue. Angus had seen frogs with proportionately smaller tongues than this thing had wriggling out of its bloody mouth.

But what got Angus to seriously considering soiling his trousers were the creature's eyes.

It didn't have any.

The monster moved out of the cop's torch beam after a second.

That was more than enough for Angus.

He ran.

"Wait!" the two-gun girl cried, but Angus ignored her and ran to the back of the church.

He'd be safe there.

"I'll get him," the bloody stupid girl said.

Turning a corner, he ran into a side area, separated from the rest of the church by a wooden screen. He saw the large birdbath-like tub, and realized this was the baptistry. Several smaller pews were set up nearby.

Suddenly, a candelabrum on the side wall fell. Angus jumped, and almost pulled the trigger on his gun. He hadn't fired it yet, but he was bloody well ready to.

But he didn't see anything.

A sound like cracking wood came from the area where the small pews were. Angus turned the gun toward the pews.

He still didn't see anything.

Bloody hell.

With a resounding crash, the baptismal font fell to the stone floor, its collapse echoing off the ceilings, holy water spilling at Angus's feet. He turned his gun on the floor where the font had fallen.

Still, he didn't see a bloody thing.

Where was the creature?

Why was it playing these games?

Angus just wanted to live.

Was that asking so much?

He turned to leave the baptistry—

—and found himself face to eyeless face with the creature he'd glimpsed before.

The tongue leapt out of its mouth and wrapped around Angus's neck.

Then it squeezed.

Angus tried desperately to lift his arm so he could fire his gun, but he was having so much trouble breathing that he couldn't make any body part behave itself properly.

The tongue started to retract, pulling him closer. Angus noted, bizarrely, that the monster had bloody wretched breath.

As soon as Angus was close enough, the creature grabbed him.

With its claws extended.

Angus had never felt pain so great in his life as he did when the monster literally tore him to pieces.

The only consolation was that it didn't last for very long.

FIFTEEN

Jill Valentine heard a dripping sound as she moved behind the wooden screen to a closed-off area of the church. She had heard a noise there, and thought that maybe the idiot had gone back there.

Or maybe it was that thing Peyton had captured in his flashlight beam for an instant.

Jill realized that she didn't even know the idiot's name. She focused on that, because focusing on anything else was just too much at this point.

Zombies walking the forests of Arklay was bad enough.

Then being suspended.

Then the same zombies stalking the streets of Raccoon.

Then Umbrella thugs shooting innocent people after cutting off their only means of escape.

And now she and Peyton were stuck in a church with a zombie, a nutty priest, a lunatic with a .357, a pain-in-the-ass reporter, and something out of a bad horror movie.

Water collected around her boots. She looked down to see that it had pooled next to a basin that had been knocked over—for baptisms, maybe?

She realized that it was probably holy water. That might prove handy if they came across vampires, an idea that seemed a lot less far-fetched than it had been twenty-four hours ago.

Whatever. That water had all spilled out. It wasn't the source of the dripping she was hearing.

Then she noticed that one of the small pews had been smashed. She caught sight of something under the wreckage.

Moving closer, she saw red mixed in with the wood, dripping off the splinters of the shattered pew.

Blood.

Peering over, she saw what was left of the idiot with the gun. Whatever that thing was Peyton had flashed the light on, it had the ability to rip a human body into remarkably small chunks.

Jill Valentine had been a police officer for all her adult life. She'd seen plenty of dead bodies in her time. The first couple had made her mildly ill, but she grew accustomed to the look, the smell, the *feel* of death. She had to if she was to do her job properly.

But this—nothing she'd seen in all her years on the RCPD had prepared her for this level of insult to the human form.

She supposed she could have searched the remains for identification so she could at least find out what this guy's name was, but Jill didn't have the stomach for it.

Especially once she did the one thing she had to force herself to have the stomach for.

Gingerly reaching down into the remains, she liberated the .357, which was still gripped by a hand that had been severed sloppily at the wrist. The weapon was covered in blood.

She turned and hurried back into the main part of the church. They *definitely* needed to stick together if there was something that could do *that* roaming around.

Questions poured into her mind. Where had that thing *come* from? It wasn't like any animal Jill was familiar with—didn't even bear a passing resemblance.

Could Umbrella have done this? Was it even possible?

Hell, zombies weren't something she'd have considered possible until Arklay. If the Corporation could make one horror-movie staple real, why not another?

Only when she got to the front of the church did she realize it was quiet—and empty.

Where the hell were Peyton and Morales?

A hand clamped on her mouth, with another grabbing her around the waist and pulling her into a niche behind the altar.

Jill broke the grip and whirled, holding up the blood-soaked .357—

—until she realized that it was Peyton who had

grabbed her. Morales was standing next to him. Peyton looked pissed; the reporter was obviously scared out of her gourd.

"Peyton," Jill started angrily, but the sergeant silenced her with a look.

He pointed at the pulpit. Jill turned and saw the creature perched on it, looking like a vulture about to pounce, its tongue waving in the air.

Just as Jill was about to ask why they were hiding here if the creature was so close, Peyton pointed at the church door.

Another of the creatures was hanging from the wall over the entrance like some kind of gecko.

Christ. Two of them.

"They got us boxed in," Peyton whispered.

Morales looked up. "What is that?"

Following her gaze, Jill saw that the Lucifer-goes-to-hell stained glass over the door was starting to glow.

Just at the moment, she really didn't appreciate the symbolism.

Then Jill almost jumped out of her skin when a third creature passed right in front of her.

The number of times she had been startled this day was really starting to get on Jill's nerves.

For whatever reason, the creature hadn't noticed them yet. Perhaps a result of its having no eyes. Whatever, Jill wasn't counting on that lasting very long. Their best bet was to stay still and quiet.

Which she and Peyton both knew instinctively.

If only the same could have been said for Morales.

Jill couldn't entirely blame Morales for turning her video camera back on. She hadn't been kidding about this footage being worth an Emmy—Christ, maybe a Pulitzer—if they got out of this alive. Hell, if Jill had had video documentation of what had happened at Arklay, she'd never have been suspended.

Unfortunately, the camera made a beeping noise when it started recording.

A noise that echoed like a gunshot in the quiet church.

The creature turned toward them.

Peyton had his weapon out before Jill could draw a breath. "Run, now!" he screamed as he started shooting at the thing.

The creature was too fast, though—it dashed up toward the roof.

Even as it did so, the one doing its gecko impersonation over the church door leapt down at them.

No, at Jill.

Before she could even raise the .357, the creature slammed into her, knocking the wind out of her and sending her crashing to the floor. The blood-slick weapon slipped from her grasp, careening across the church floor under a pew.

Jill gasped for breath and rolled onto hands and knees, groping for one of her automatics. Nearby, Peyton tried to shoot the creature that had taken her down, but its tongue snapped out like a snake and knocked his weapon from his hand.

Then Peyton looked up. Jill followed his gaze.

The glow in the stained glass had grown brighter. And she could hear the sound of an engine.

No, not just any engine—a Harley.

Jill smiled.

"Down!" Peyton cried, but Jill was already ducking.

With a crash that resounded through the old church like an A-bomb, the stained glass shattered into thousands of pieces, the victim of a Harley-Davidson motorcycle impacting it at high speed.

The bike slammed right into the creature, body-checking it and sending it flying across the church.

Pain wracked Jill's chest, and she was having trouble breathing, much less getting to her feet. As she struggled to catch her breath, she tried to get a good look at their rescuer.

He wasn't what Jill expected.

For starters, he was a she. Such Harleys usually were ridden by large, middle-aged white men. The skinnier variety generally weighed upwards of three hundred pounds, and they tended toward facial hair that made the front men for ZZ Top look clean shaven.

But this Harley was driven by an athletic-looking white woman with dirty blond hair, a shotgun in a back holster, one nickel-plated Uzi on each hip, and a Colt .45 in a shoulder holster.

She was also wearing only a hospital gown with a white lab coat over it.

On any other day, Jill would have found this weird.

The woman looked at Jill with ice blue eyes and said one word.

"Move."

Morales certainly didn't need to be told twice. She ran for the front doors like a bat out of hell, Peyton limping along behind her, while Jill was still struggling to rise.

That turned out to be a huge tactical error.

On the other side of the doors that Morales opened was a teeming mass of zombies, all wanting to get in and chow down on what few living were left.

Peyton came to her rescue, and the pair of them slammed the doors shut.

The front door was certainly not an option.

Meanwhile, Biker Lady revved her Harley to a point that had to be way past the red line, then put it in gear—but with her bare feet planted on the floor.

The bike shot out from between her legs—another bit of symbolism Jill could have done without—straight into one of the creatures.

Both the creature and the Harley went flying into the air.

Biker Lady pulled her Colt and fired a single shot.

Just as Jill was wondering how this woman thought one bullet was going to stop this thing, she saw the bullet hit the Harley's gas tank.

And then the bike exploded, taking the creature and a good chunk of the altar, pulpit, lectern, and candles with it.

The third creature dropped from the ceiling, but Biker Lady was ready for this one, too. Whipping out both Uzis, she unloaded dozens of rounds into the creature as it fell.

When it hit the floor, it didn't get up.

Jill felt her breathing getting under control. She started to get up. It had been maybe ten seconds since the Harley had crashed through the stained glass.

The first creature, the one that had been body-checked by the Harley's arrival, got up and charged Biker Lady from behind.

Before Jill could gasp out a warning or unholster one of her automatics, Biker Lady gave one of the pews a hard kick.

Jill had opened her mouth to yell the warning, and now it just hung open in stupefaction as the pew went sliding across the church directly at the creature.

Everything Biker Lady had done up until now was at least within the realm of possibility. That kind of skill with a motorcycle, that good a shot, that fast a draw—all things Jill had encountered in real life. Hell, Jill herself was at least as good a shot as this woman, if not better.

But knocking a pew that was attached to the floor across a room with a single kick?

That was impossible.

Of course, so were walking dead people and eyeless, skinless creatures with tongues the size of boa constrictors.

Said creatures also had a good survival instinct—the thing leapt into the air over the pew.

However, that gave Biker Lady a clear shot. She unholstered the shotgun from her back, pumped it, and shot the creature right in the chest.

As the creature flew into the wall, Jill got to her feet,

but she didn't do anything. At this point, she was content to enjoy the show.

Biker Lady reholstered the shotgun and drew her Colt.

None of the shots hit the creature. After a second, Jill, a crack shot in her own right, realized that the woman had nonetheless hit everything she was aiming at.

The creature got up and, the wound in its chest notwithstanding, started charging Biker Lady.

For her part, the woman holstered her Colt and turned her back on the creature.

Just as the thing charged, the cross that had been hanging over the altar—until Biker Lady shot out its supports—plummeted to the floor, impaling the creature.

Amazingly, that didn't kill it, at least not right away. The creature roared and its tongue flicked out at Biker Lady.

Cool as the proverbial cucumber, Biker Lady whipped out her shotgun again and shot the thing in the face.

Jill finally found her voice.

"Who the fuck *are* you?"

"My name's Alice. We're not safe in here. That fire will spread."

Somehow, Jill restrained herself from pointing out that if this Alice woman hadn't blown up the Harley in the first place, there wouldn't *be* a fire.

Peyton muttered, "No shit." Louder, he said, "I'm

Sergeant Peyton Wells of S.T.A.R.S. This is one of my best people, Officer Jill Valentine."

"I'm impressed that you stayed in town."

Jill decided not to share her life story. "Protect and serve, that's what we do."

Alice looked at Jill. "Weren't you suspended?"

"Yeah. I saw zombies in the Arklay Mountains forest. Everyone thought I was crazy."

"At this point," Peyton said, "we're all a little crazy." He pointed to Morales, who was popping some pills from a little case she'd pulled out. "Case in point: Terri Morales, Raccoon 7 weather girl and total basket case."

Alice barely acknowledged Morales's presence. Instead, she unholstered her Colt and moved quickly, gracefully toward the rear of the church.

Jill walked over to Peyton and offered her arm. The sergeant was looking even paler.

"You look like shit, Peyton."

"Good," Peyton said, taking her hand. "I'd hate to feel this way and not look the part."

As she helped Peyton hobble to the rear of the church, Jill turned and looked at Morales. She was filming the flaming wreckage of the Harley.

"You coming, weathergirl?"

"Yeah, yeah," Morales said. "This is gonna make one *helluva* story."

SIXTEEN

Until she pulled her Harley onto Dilmore Place, Alice had thought that the only thing she had to worry about were the undead creatures.

Then she sensed the lickers.

The genetically engineered monstrosities were housed in tanks in a room in the Hive that the official specs designated as a dining hall. The irony hadn't been lost on Alice: the *things* inside the room would eat pretty much anything.

Or, more to the point, any*one*.

The Red Queen had freed one of the lickers as a backup plan in case she wasn't able to contain the T-virus. The thing had killed Spence (who deserved it) and Kaplan (who really didn't) before Alice and Matt had been able to dispatch it—barely.

But until she sensed the presence of three of the things in the church, she'd had no idea that any of the others had gotten out as well.

Nor had she any idea that she *could* sense their presence.

Again, she wondered just what the fuck they'd done to her after they took her and Matt.

Not to mention what had happened to Matt.

As if the undead weren't enough.

After she'd taken care of them, she found she had more people to babysit. Still, she couldn't just leave Valentine, Wells, and Morales to die. So she led them into the graveyard in the back. The church would be kindling before long.

"How'd you wind up in here?" Alice asked.

"Well, we tried leaving the city, but Umbrella sealed off the Ravens' Gate," Valentine said. "Put up a nice big wall to keep the riffraff in. Anyone approaching the wall was shot on sight. Repeatedly."

"So you came to a church?"

Valentine shrugged. "We're not really overburdened with alternatives. We figured we'd be safe in there. We were wrong."

"And what the fuck are we doing *here?*" Morales asked while popping an indeterminate number of pills that she probably shouldn't have been taking together. "Hello? Has anyone noticed? We're in a *graveyard*, people!"

Alice supposed that those keen powers of observation were why she was a reporter. But she said nothing.

Valentine and Wells, at least, would be of use, being trained. Morales was dead weight.

Then it started raining.

One month ago, Alice had been the head of security for the Hive, living a good life with a hefty paycheck, sharing a house with a fake husband with whom she had excellent sex. Yes, she worked for bastards, but she was working on ways to deal with that, and at least she knew her position was more or less secure and her life more or less made sense.

Now she was walking through a muddy graveyard in the rain, wearing only a hospital gown, a lab coat, and enough firepower to take on an army squadron, facing off against the undead citizens of Raccoon City and a pack of genetically engineered monsters.

Funny how much could change in a month.

The graveyard was fenced in on three sides by a wrought-iron fence, and on the fourth by the church itself. The fire would probably keep that fourth side safe, and two of the fence sides were clear, but more and more undead were banging up against the fence on the Lyons Street side. Sooner or later, they'd probably break through.

Morales walked up to her, the rain causing her makeup to run. Her caking mascara gave her a look that matched the animal for whom the city was named.

"What's the plan?" the reporter asked.

"Stay alive."

Morales blinked. "That's it?"

"That's it."

The reporter shook her head. "Nice plan. Should I paint a bull's-eye on my face?"

"Suit yourself."

"We have to stop for a moment," said Valentine from behind them.

Alice turned to see that Wells was barely able to walk from the wound in his leg. It had been bound expertly, but it still didn't look good.

"I don't think that's a good idea," Morales said. "There may be more of those things."

Shaking her head, Alice said, "They hunt in packs. If there were more, we'd have seen them by now."

Morales whirled back to look at Alice with her raccoon eyes. Her demeanor was now that of an inquisitive reporter. "So you *do* know what they are?"

There was no reason to conceal it. "Bioweapons, from the Umbrella labs beneath the city."

"How come you know so much about Umbrella?" Valentine asked, sounding understandably suspicious.

"I used to work for them—before I learned the error of my ways."

Before Valentine could say anything else, Wells cried out in pain. "Dammit!"

The wound was starting to bleed again.

Alice let out a long breath.

"You're infected."

"Don't worry about me."

It wasn't Wells that Alice was worried about. She unholstered her Colt.

Moving faster than Alice would have believed possible from someone who wasn't Alice herself, Valentine drew one of her own weapons and pointed it right at Alice's head. "Hold it!"

Wells pulled out his own weapon and pointed it at Alice.

Alice drew one of her Uzis and pointed it at Valentine.

Morales, naturally, raised her camera to make sure she got all of this on tape. Not that Alice could entirely blame her. What reporter could resist a front-row seat for a good old-fashioned Mexican standoff?

"What do you think you're doing?" Valentine asked.

It was probably the stupidest thing she could have said. "He's *wounded,*" Alice said slowly. "The infection's spreading."

"I'm fine," Wells said.

He sounded as awful as Rain had when she insisted she was still okay. She'd died on the train, when they were only minutes from making it out. Matt had had to shoot her in the head.

Alice looked at Valentine. "You should take care of him now."

She almost added: *Like I didn't take care of Rain when I had the chance.*

"He's my friend." Valentine had yet to lower her pistol.

"I understand," Alice said, meaning it wholeheartedly, "but it'll be more difficult later. You know that." Then she cocked her Colt.

"No!" Valentine cried, doing the same with her

weapon. "If it comes to that—I'll take care of it myself."

Unbidden, Alice thought back to the train, just before the licker had attacked, when she, Matt, Kaplan, and Rain thought they were home free.

"I don't want to be one of those things," Rain had said, *"walking around without a soul. When the time comes, you'll take care of it."*

Valentine and Wells had that bond law-enforcement officers had. Alice had seen it during her abortive time in the Treasury Department, before the government agency's sexism drove her to Umbrella's waiting, and high-paying, arms.

She lowered her weapons.

"As you wish."

Only then did Valentine lower hers.

Alice turned to Wells.

"It's nothing personal. But in an hour, maybe two, you'll be dead. Then, minutes later, you'll be one of them. You'll endanger your friends, try to kill them— maybe succeed. Sorry, but that's just the way it is."

Before the shocked-looking Wells could form a reply, they were all startled by the sound of wrenching metal.

The undead were breaking through the fence.

Morales, of course, was filming with that camera of hers. Alice noted with some sliver of amusement that the camera had been manufactured by one of Umbrella's subsidiaries.

Luckily, the undead hadn't really focused on the four of them yet, and they still moved ridiculously slowly. It was the living's best advantage: speed.

Then Morales screamed.

Alice looked over to see that the reporter was being pulled down into the mud by the occupant of one of the graves.

The T-virus had gotten into the ground.

Valentine pulled Morales free even as Wells drew his weapon.

Alice put a hand on his arm. "Save your ammo."

Then she dispatched the undead with a swift kick to its head, breaking its neck.

"These things react to sound. Use your guns and we'll just attract more of them."

"You really think that matters?" Valentine asked, looking past Alice.

Dozens of undead were coming in from Lyons Street. Dozens more were rising from their graves.

Then Alice moved.

Valentine took a couple down, and Wells might have gotten one. Morales just stood filming everything.

Alice took out the rest of them.

It was an odd feeling—kind of like *Zen and the Art of Killing Zombies*. She didn't really need to think about what she was doing, she simply let her instincts take hold. Whatever Cain's science goons had done to her had taken her natural athleticism and her years of training and raised them both several orders of magnitude.

Even as she snapped one undead's neck with her arms, her legs were planting her feet for a spin-kick that would shatter the spine of another, then her hand slammed into the throat of a third, then she broke the leg of a fourth with a kick that set it up to have its neck broken—all in the time it took Valentine to throw one punch.

When there was only one left, Alice smashed its head into a gravestone, right into the words **REST IN PEACE.**

Valentine was giving Alice a look that was both furious and curious.

However, for the moment, all she did was indicate Alice's final victim and the words on the gravestone. "I've really had enough irony for one day."

Alice cracked a slight smile at that.

"Let's move."

There was a gate on the far side that led to Killiany Way, a small side street that emptied onto Swann Road, a larger street and therefore easier to defend oneself on, but not so busy that it was likely to be packed to the gills with undead.

The rain had stopped, and the sky was clearing. The moon was about three-quarters full and that, along with the occasional burning car, provided the only illumination for the foursome as they wended their way toward Swann.

"Where are we going?" Morales asked.

Alice looked up, realizing that this was perhaps the wrong way to go.

Sitting on the corner of Killiany and Swann was an imposing brick edifice with a large sign carved into the stonework over the front entrance:

CITY MORGUE.

In response to Morales's question, Alice said, "The hell away from here."

They turned onto Swann. Alice stayed on the double yellow line, the others following her.

"No signal."

Alice turned to see Wells trying to use a cell phone. He kept putting it to his ear, then staring accusingly at the display. She almost laughed.

"No reception at all."

"Someone's jamming it," Alice said.

"Who?"

"Umbrella. They want to keep news of what's happening here from getting out."

"Not if I have anything to say about it," Morales muttered. She wandered to the sidewalk to film one of the looted buildings.

"Stay in the middle of the street," Alice called out. "Keep away from enclosed spaces. Most of those things are slow. We'll be better off in the open."

To Alice's surprise, Morales listened to her. She supposed that her ass-kicking of the undead had gained her some respect.

She shook her head. Ass-Kicking Alice—that had been her nickname in Security Division. Looked like she'd really earned it now.

Morales pulled out another bottle of pills. This time, Alice took pity on her—besides, if they were going to get out of this, they needed to have all their faculties about them. Alice wasn't worried in the least about Valentine, and Wells wouldn't be a factor for very long—if Valentine couldn't kill him, Alice would—but Morales needed to be at what passed for her best.

So Alice knocked the pill bottle to the wet pavement.

"Don't take these. They're not good for you." She smiled. "I know a few things about pharmaceuticals."

Morales looked stunned for a minute, then nodded.

"Yes—yes, of course—you're right."

Alice turned to move forward. Behind her, Valentine was giving her another one of her furious/curious looks. The fact that Alice didn't need to look to know this frightened her—yet another notch for Cain's ledger.

"What are you staring at?" she asked

"I'm not sure." Valentine fell into step beside Alice. "Those were some pretty slick moves back there. I'm good—some might say the best. But I'm not that good."

"You should be thankful for that," Alice said quietly.

"What do you mean?"

"They did something to me."

With a start, Alice realized that that was really all she could say. She had no trouble trusting Valentine, given what they were all going through—and that they'd likely all be dead by morning—but she really didn't know anything beyond that Cain and his goons had done *something* to her.

As they passed a pay phone, it started ringing.

"Let's keep moving before the sound attracts anything," Alice said, picking up the pace.

Valentine kept up with her, Morales and Wells lagging behind.

The ringing stopped as soon as they were past the pay phone.

Weird.

Then, as they passed a mostly looted deli, the pay phone next to its front door started to ring.

"Keep going," Alice said, not liking this one bit.

Again, the ringing stopped once they passed it.

"Is it just me," Morales said, "or is this a little weird?"

They reached an intersection, and suddenly it was like the chimes of Big Ben in phone ringing: every pay phone in sight started sounding off.

After three or four rings, they all stopped—

—except for the one next to a burned-out diner.

It wouldn't stop ringing.

"Call it a hunch," Valentine said, "but I think someone wants to talk to us."

Alice agreed. She went over and gingerly picked up the phone. Next to her, Valentine unholstered her pistol.

"Hello?"

"I thought you were never going to answer," said a male voice on the other end.

"Who is this?"

"I can get you out of the city. All four of you."

Alice put her hand over the mouthpiece and said to Valentine, "He can see us."

The man on the other end continued. "But first, we have to come to an arrangement. Are you ready to make a deal?"

Valentine immediately started a systematic check of

the area to see where this guy was hiding. Alice admired the efficiency, but it was a waste. A glance across the street revealed how this man could see them.

"Are you ready to make a deal?" the man repeated.

"Do we have a choice?"

A bitter chuckle sounded through the earpiece. "Not if you want to live beyond tonight."

Valentine finished her search. She mouthed the words, "There's no one there."

Pointing across the street, Alice indicated the surveillance camera over the intersection. Used primarily to monitor traffic infractions, the network of cameras had been installed by Umbrella three years earlier under contract to the RCPD.

"What is your answer?" the man asked.

From what Valentine had told her, getting out of the city was damn near impossible. Umbrella would have every outgoing artery sealed off, and it was just like Cain to tell his people to use deadly force on innocent people.

Asshole.

Like she'd indicated in her question to their caller, they didn't have a choice.

"Tell me more."

SEVEN†EEN

Never in his life had Carlos Olivera seen anything like this. If he lived to be a hundred, he doubted he'd ever see anything like this again.

Then again, his living to see even tomorrow morning was looking doubtful in the extreme.

Jorge was definitely right: zombies were scarier. Especially when hundreds of them were shuffling toward him and his team in almost perfectly choreographed unison, dozens of pale, sickly, watery-eyed, black-toothed animated corpses with but a single thought.

Chow down on Carlos and his people.

Askegren had been killed when they first made it onto the street from the roof where Carlos had failed to rescue the blond woman.

Carter had been wounded when one of the zombies

bit his arm, and he could barely hold up his MP5K.

Carlos, Loginov, O'Neill, and Nicholai were trying to shoot the things in the head, but there were so many of them. . . .

Laying down suppressing fire, Carlos cried, "Fall back! I said, fall back!"

Even as they moved back toward Main Street, another surge of zombies came out from an alley, cutting Loginov off from the rest of them.

"Dammit! Yuri!" Carlos raced into the mass of zombies. He'd already lost one man; he wasn't losing anyone else.

Just as he had on the roof, Carlos unloaded both his Colts into the mass of zombies trying to eat Loginov alive.

That wiped out enough of them that Carlos was able to get the now-wounded Loginov out of the crowd and help him toward the remainder of the team.

Standing in his way was Askegren. Blood covered his face from the massive head wound that had killed him, but apparently whatever part of his brain the T-virus had activated was still intact.

J.P. Askegren had been an officer with the Prince Georges County Sheriff's Department, but, as he often joked, he'd left "because I passed the IQ test." There was, Askegren felt, too much of the southern redneck in that particular border state, or at least in the sheriff's office, and he got tired of dealing with people whose loftiest goal was "to see how many niggers they could bust before lunchtime."

Six months after he'd quit in disgust, his wife got a job offer from a company in Raccoon City, and they'd moved. Cain had hired him and assigned him to Carlos's unit. He was a good man and a loving husband, and was three months away from being a good father.

Or, rather, he had been until this morning. They had no idea what had happened to his six-months-pregnant wife.

And now, Carlos had to shoot him in the head.

"Definitely the worst vacation of my life," Carlos muttered. It was such a nice cabin, too. . . .

He caught up to the rest of the team just as Carter leaned in and bit O'Neill on the neck.

Any other day, Carlos would have reprimanded the two of them for public displays of affection.

Today, it just meant that one of them was dead, and the other would be soon.

Before Carlos could do anything, O'Neill grabbed her lover's head and snapped his neck.

"Fuck," she said, putting her hand to her neck, then looking at the blood pooled on it.

Without hesitating, she pulled out her Beretta and shoved the barrel in her mouth.

"No!" Carlos screamed, but it was too late. Sam O'Neill's blood and brains splattered in a wide pattern across the wall behind her and her body fell to the pavement next to Jack Carter's.

Carlos looked around to see no zombies left, but only Nicholai still standing.

"Where's Halprin?"

Nicholai pointed at the ground, where Halprin lay with her head at an impossible angle.

"Jack went after the medic first. She pushed him off, fell, and broke her neck."

Loginov, a devout Catholic—which was why he'd left the Soviet Union twenty years ago—made the sign of the cross. "At—at least she won't come back—as one of those—those *things*."

"That's not a helluva lot of consolation." Carlos looked down the street. More zombies were massing and heading their way. "Let's move."

Maneuvering amid the abandoned and burning cars and the cracked pavement, Carlos led the two Russians to a back alley where a streetcar had gone off the rails and crashed into a wall.

When they got inside, making sure that no zombies were hiding out, Carlos took a look at Loginov's wound, pulling a field bandage out of one of the pouches on his uniform.

Within a few minutes, he'd tied it off. "I've stopped the bleeding."

He looked up to see that Loginov was losing consciousness.

"Hey. Hey! Stay awake. You have to stay conscious, understand?"

"Yeah." But Loginov was still drifting off.

Carlos snapped. "Pay attention, soldier!"

Now Loginov's eyes snapped into focus. "I get it. I'm okay—I'm okay."

He didn't sound okay. He sounded like he was about

to keel over and die, which fit because he *looked* like he was going to keel over and die.

But at least he was awake.

"Good."

"Thank you—for coming back."

"You'd do the same for me." Carlos almost added that he had to save *somebody* today, but didn't. That way lay madness. "Now, stay focused, you got it?"

Loginov managed a ragged smile. "Yes, sir."

Nicholai, meanwhile, was trying to raise someone— anyone—on the radio.

"Alpha team to base, this is alpha team to base. Come in, base. Come in, base. Dammit!" He looked over at Carlos. "Why don't they reply? They can't just *leave* us in here. Why don't they evac us?"

Carlos had always been honest with his people, and he saw no reason to stop now. So rather than give some kind of crap answer that would sound unconvincingly reassuring, he simply said, "I don't know."

"Why did they even send us *in* here?"

Nicholai started pacing the streetcar, more agitated than Carlos had ever seen him—indeed, more agitated than Carlos had thought him capable of being.

"We never stood a chance. We weren't trained for this—*nobody*'s been trained for this! We never—"

"Wait." Carlos interrupted Nicholai's rant at a familiar sound.

He stood up.

"What?" Nicholai asked.

"Listen."

It was a helicopter.

Lipinski had been instructed to return to base after dropping them off, so they were stuck without evac in this mess. Maybe now, though, they'd be picked up.

"Thank God!" Nicholai moved faster than Carlos had ever seen the big man move, and ran out into the street. "They've come for us. Thank God!"

Carlos followed at a more leisurely pace, as did Loginov, to find the big man waving his arms at a C89 overhead. The helicopter and several others like it had been purchased from the Russian government by Umbrella, and were now emblazoned with the company's stylized logo.

"Down here! We're down here! *Down here!*"

But the helicopter just flew on by.

Nicholai shot Carlos a look. "What are they doing?"

Carlos, however, kept his eye on the helicopter. "They're landing over there."

Without even having to consult each other, they each took one of Loginov's arms and wrapped it around their respective shoulders. The trio then hobbled in the direction the helicopter was moving.

As they turned the corner of Main onto Johnson Avenue, Carlos realized where the helicopter was probably going: the Raccoon City Hospital. The company had donated a wing to the hospital, and used it for some of its medical work.

Nicholai was trying to cheer up his countryman.

"It's going to be okay, Yuri. We're going to fix you

up, then we're going to get drunk. We're going to party."

Carlos snorted. Yuri Loginov might be a devout Catholic, but he had the drinking habits of a devout Muslim, to wit, none. Not for lack of trying on Nicholai's part, of course.

Just as they came within sight of the hospital, Carlos saw that the helicopter was hovering over the hospital's atrium, shining a light into one of the windows.

Nicholai started waving again, leaving Carlos to support Loginov alone.

"We're over here!"

Someone inside the helicopter tossed two heavy-duty flight cases through one of the windows. The crash of the glass was barely audible over the rotors of the helicopter, which then turned and flew off.

"No! Don't leave!" Nicholai was now jumping up and down, still waving his arms. "We're coming! We're down here!"

Once the helicopter was out of sight, Nicholai turned angrily toward Carlos.

"They dropped something inside the hospital. Did you see it?"

Carlos nodded.

"Maybe a radio? One that *works?*"

"Worth looking," Carlos said. "Let's go."

They entered the hospital, Nicholai and Carlos once again supporting the injured Loginov.

The place was deserted. No doctors, no nurses, no patients.

At least the power was still on. The hospital's own

generators were probably still functioning, even if Raccoon's grid was mostly down.

They worked their way to the atrium. In the midst of the potted palms, giant ferns, and other ugly plant life that someone inexplicably thought would soothe the sick were two heavy-duty weapons cases.

Big heavy-duty weapons cases.

They set Loginov—who was drifting in and out of consciousness—against one of the palms.

"What the hell is this?" Nicholai asked.

The cases were empty.

"Looks like weapons cases."

"We don't need weapons, we need an evac!"

"This wasn't for us."

Carlos looked at Nicholai. Someone had already opened these massive cases and taken out whatever was inside them.

Someone who was probably still there.

Instinctively, Carlos looked up.

For a brief instant, he saw a massive silhouette of what looked like a tank on legs.

Then it was gone.

Carlos looked at Nicholai.

Nicholai looked at Carlos.

Then Carlos felt massive pain, as Yuri Loginov—or, rather, Yuri Loginov's corpse—bit into his shoulder.

Carlos punched his subordinate in the face, which got the biting to stop. Then he grabbed Loginov's head and twisted.

The snap of bone followed a second later.

The Russian fell to the floor in a twisted heap.

Nicholai looked sadly down at the corpse.

"I guess I won't be getting him drunk."

"Let's go," Carlos said.

"A pity—I bet he'd have made a good drunk."

More urgently, Carlos repeated, "Let's *go*."

"I'll have to get drunk for both of us."

Putting a hand on his second's shoulder, Carlos said, *"Nicholai!* Focus! We're in a hospital, they're bound to have a first-aid kit or three that's better than our field pack. Let's find it before I bleed out here, okay?"

"Yes—yes, right, of course." Nicholai shook his head. "Let us go."

It didn't take long for them to get to the ambulance bay and start rifling through an abandoned ambulance for supplies. Most of the supplies in the hospital itself had turned out to be either stolen, damaged, or tainted. But this ambo, at least, was intact. Carlos was grateful for that.

Unfortunately, nothing he did to try to stop the bleeding where Loginov had bitten his shoulder seemed to be doing any good. The wound would not clot for anything.

Which meant there was a very good chance Carlos himself was going to become one of Jorge's scary zombies.

Definitely a crappy vacation.

"It won't stop bleeding," he said, as much to engage Nicholai in conversation as anything.

"How could they have missed us?" Nicholai asked.

"What?"

"The chopper. We were right there in the street, in front of the hospital. How could they not have seen us?"

Carlos sighed and said out loud what he'd been afraid to admit up until now.

"They saw us."

"What do you mean?"

Standing and putting his uninjured hand on Nicholai's shoulder, Carlos said, "We're assets, Nicholai. Expendable assets. And we just got expended."

Before they could discuss the subject further, the pay phone in the ambulance bay, an abandoned cell phone in the passenger seat of the ambo, and several phones in smashed window of the Motorola store across the street began to ring, all at the same time.

Carlos looked at Nicholai in confusion.

EİGHTEEП

Nemesis activated.

All systems came online one after another.

The flow of drugs ceased.

His head cleared.

An eye opened. Then the other.

Nemesis took in his surroundings.

As he did, he tried to remember who he was.

Wait, that was ridiculous. He knew who he was: Nemesis. All he needed now were instructions from his masters at the Umbrella Corporation. They had built him, and they directed him.

No!

A voice screamed in his mind.

The voice was familiar, yet wholly unknown.

I am not a tool of Umbrella! I'm trying to destroy them!

Destroy them? What an absurd notion. He was Nemesis. His sole function in life was to do the bidding of the Umbrella Corporation.

Nemesis rose from his bed. He looked around the room, identifying it as a hospital. In addition to the usual colors and textures, he could determine how hot or cold something was, and any ultraviolet radiation was enough to allow him to make out shapes.

My God, how is this possible? I can see in infrared and *ultraviolet.*

Again, Nemesis was confused. This voice was still in his mind, but he did not recognize it.

I'm Matthew Addison! I was supposed to meet with my sister, Lisa Broward. She was going to provide me with information that would expose the Umbrella Corporation's illegal activities. Instead, I got caught up in a nightmare scenario. An entire underground complex of Umbrella's, including five hundred people, was destroyed. I watched people die, even killed some myself—and ended up infected with the same T-virus that killed the Umbrella employees. I don't remember what happened after that. What did they do to me?

Nemesis disregarded the voice. It made no sense.

The heads-up display in one corner of his visual range scrolled across with text.

ALL SYSTEMS ACTIVATED.

Then Nemesis received more instructions. No words came to him, he simply *knew* what he had to do next.

Christ, are they broadcasting right into my skull?

Nemesis walked to the door. A large hand turned the knob.

My God, how'd my hand get that big? And what the fuck are all these tubes and wires?

Walking with a heavy tread that felt like it was straining the floor's ability to carry his weight, Nemesis proceeded to the atrium, knowing the most direct route from the Umbrella wing, even though he'd never set foot in this hospital before now.

In fact, he'd never set foot anywhere before now. He had no memory of anything prior to awakening in the hospital.

Dammit, that's not true! I'm Matt Addison! I'm a human being, goddammit, and you can't take my body—my life—away from me like this! Let me the fuck out of this!

Nemesis realized that this was some remnant of the template. Or perhaps a phantom program in his memory core. Regardless, he would ignore it until it went away.

Walking past a broken window, Nemesis found two large cases on the floor of the atrium. He bent over and opened one of them.

Jesus fucking Christ, that's a big rocket launcher. I've never seen anything that large. How could anyone hold that?

Nemesis picked up the rocket launcher. About seven feet in length, it had a shoulder strap. He slung it over his shoulder as easily as he might a backpack.

What the fuck did they do to me?

The second case contained a rail gun.

That's one of those things they mount on helicopters.

Nemesis picked it up with one giant hand.

Then he proceeded to the egress.

DIRECTIVE: PROCEED THROUGH RACCOON CITY.

Nemesis saw a few people in the hospital, but they gave off no heat, so they were obviously undead who had been animated by the T-virus. They were not threats, and he had been given no directive to engage them.

So he ignored them.

He briefly caught sight of two men being attacked by a third. The two men were alive, the third was not. But again, he received no directives to engage them, so he ignored them and continued to the streets.

What the fuck is going on? Those guys down there are wearing the same outfits that Rain, Kaplan, and the rest of them were wearing. They've gotta be more of Umbrella's goon squad.

Nemesis walked outside.

He saw several abandoned, damaged motor vehicles of a variety of types, ranging from trucks to sport-utility vehicles to buses to sedans to motorcycles, and others. Many windows had been compromised, and broken glass littered the streets, as did blood.

He looked around and found no indications of life beyond a rat or two.

I don't believe it. The fuckers opened the Hive back up and let the zombie workers out. Just when I thought Umbrella couldn't possibly get any more despicable . . .

Nemesis continued down the street. Any impediments, regardless of size, were brushed aside or crushed. Nothing stood in his way.

Nor could it. He was Nemesis. Created by the Umbrella Corporation to be the perfect fighting machine.

He turned a corner from Johnson Avenue onto Main Street. In the distance, he saw several of the deceased people animated by the T-virus. He could also hear a human voice speaking.

"Come and get it."

One of the deceased people was hit with a bullet fired from a shotgun.

"Plenty to go 'round."

Another deceased person was hit with a bullet. Neither deceased person had much of a head remaining.

"That's right, roll up, roll up."

Nemesis found the source of the voice by triangulating the sound with the trajectories of the bullets. It was a man standing on the roof of an establishment called Grady's Inn. His uniform identified him as a member of the Special Tactics and Rescue Squad of the Raccoon City Police Department, though he also wore a large ten-gallon cowboy hat that was not officially part of the dress code.

Even as Nemesis moved closer to the S.T.A.R.S. sniper, the sniper also saw him.

"What the fuck is that?"

Jesus Christ, asshole, get off the damn roof before I kill you! And why the fuck are you up there playing duck shoot with the zombies? This is your idea of protecting and serving? I can't believe I pretended to be one of you RCPD asswipes.

Nemesis detected several more heat signatures in a nearby store called Mostly Colt, an emporium that specialized in the sale of hand weaponry. As he walked past, he saw that most of them also wore the uniform of S.T.A.R.S.

A shotgun bullet hit him in the chest.

Holy shit. I just got shot, but it felt like a mild tap on the ribs. What the fuck did they fucking do *to me?*

"I must've missed," said the sniper from his vantage point. "I never miss."

You didn't, jackass, now get out *of there!*

DIRECTIVE: SEEK AND DESTROY MEMBERS OF S.T.A.R.S.

Fuck, no. No, don't make me do this.

He could hear the shell being placed into the breech, the clack of metal on metal as the sniper loaded the fresh ammunition.

"Son of a bitch! You're going down!"

Nemesis raised the rail gun, holding up the massive weapon like it was a six-shooter.

It's like it doesn't weigh a thing. God . . .

The sniper hesitated at the sight of the rail gun being aimed at him.

Yeah, I'd fucking hesitate, too.

"Shit!"

Hundreds of shells exploded around the roof of Grady's Inn. But Nemesis still detected the sniper from the heat he gave off. He was still alive and had taken cover behind the roof access cabin.

Nemesis continued firing the rail gun with one hand.

With his other, and without a single hesitation in the discharge of the other weapon, he raised the rocket launcher onto his shoulder and fired a missile at the roof of Grady's Inn.

A moment later, the entire inn was one massive heat signature as it exploded from the missile's impact.

Nemesis lowered his weapons, having accomplished his most recent directive.

Oh, God...

Then Nemesis turned toward Mostly Colt.

ΠΙΝΕΤΕΕΠ

"What do we have?" Cain asked Johanssen.

The young tech looked up at the major as he approached. Karl Johanssen was one of the primary techheads assigned to the Nemesis Program, and the only one Cain could stand to talk to. Johanssen had served for two tours in the U.S. Marine Corps before taking the job with Umbrella. True, he was a jarhead asswipe, but that still made him easier to talk to than the other, much bigger asswipes in the Nemesis Program. None of them was quite at the same level of irritation as Ashford. However, while Cain had to be nice to Ashford, he was under no obligation to be the same for the scientists, technicians, and other head-in-the-clouds jackasses.

Johanssen, though, understood things like chain of command and how to follow an order. So he was the liaison between the program and Cain himself. With Nemesis now up and running, Cain had ordered Johanssen to be the one handling the board while he was active.

The head of the Nemesis Program, an irritating little twerp named Sam Isaacs, objected to this, saying that *he* should be the one to run it, since *he* knew the program better than anyone, and, while he had nothing but the utmost respect for Mr. Johanssen, it would really make a great deal more sense for Isaacs to be running the board.

Cain told Isaacs to go fuck himself, and instructed Johanssen to run the board.

This meant that Johanssen had access to Nemesis's sight, shown on a plasma-screen monitor; his hearing, piped through top-of-the-line speakers from PerryMyk (a subsidiary of Umbrella); his vital signs, displayed on another plasma screen; and his brain, via a computer terminal with an ergonomic keyboard that fed directly into his cerebral cortex.

Right now, the sight monitor was showing a gun shop and several heat signatures. Since the undead didn't show up on infrared, that meant living beings.

In response to Cain's question, Johanssen said, "A dozen armed men, well organized."

Cain shook his head. "I'm surprised there's anyone left alive."

"They're S.T.A.R.S.," Johanssen said. "Raccoon City's S.W.A.T. team, basically. They're the best."

"The best." Cain snorted. One and his team were the best. These guys were just glorified beat cops who got to play with nicer toys. "Let's see how good they really are."

Johanssen nodded in understanding. That was another reason why Cain liked Johanssen—he understood what Cain told him without having to have it explained several dozen times. And it wasn't as if there were any moral issues. Anyone still in Raccoon City was as good as dead—if the T-virus didn't get them, tomorrow morning's cleansing would—so what difference did it make how they died?

Life was, after all, cheap.

"Altering protocols." With those words, Johanssen wheeled his chair over to the ergonomic keyboard and started typing in commands.

The directive prompt came up on the monitor, and Johanssen typed in: SEEK AND DESTROY MEMBERS OF S.T.A.R.S.

While he did so, Cain watched the monitor. The computer had identified most of the people in the gun shop from their RCPD uniforms. One in civilian clothes was Ryan Henderson, the captain in charge of S.T.A.R.S. Operations. The remaining two were probably officers who were off duty when all hell broke loose, or maybe civilians the others were protecting.

Nemesis then found a S.T.A.R.S. sniper on the roof of a nearby building.

Cain looked over to see that Johanssen was calling up face ID on the sniper. He was a S.T.A.R.S. sharpshooter named Michael Guthrie, originally from Texas—which explained the out-of-uniform cowboy hat he wore—who had been reprimanded four times for excessive force.

Predictably, Guthrie took a shot at Nemesis as soon as he came into sight.

Just as predictably, it had no appreciable effect on Nemesis.

Oh, there was *an* effect—but Cain only knew that because of what the other monitors in front of him were displaying.

Verifying the information on the monitors, Johanssen said, "Point-zero-one percent damage. Regenerating at a cellular level."

Cain nodded. Just as Isaacs had said, Nemesis's metabolism was sufficiently supercharged that he could regenerate tissue to heal any wound.

Johanssen looked up at Cain. "Secondary directive established. Nemesis will now target anyone recognized as S.T.A.R.S." Johanssen hesitated. "Sir, that means he won't target the other two people in the gun shop—unless they physically threaten him."

"That's all right, son," Cain said with a small smile. "I'd say there's a good chance of the latter, wouldn't you?"

"Yes, sir."

Even as those two words came out of Johanssen's mouth, the monitor that fed into the Umbrella-made RCPD traffic camera showed Nemesis raising the rail gun.

What a sight it was.

Although, strictly speaking, the body of Nemesis

originally had belonged to a jackass troublemaker named Matthew Addison, said body was now barely recognizable as his.

Still, for whatever reason, Addison's DNA was particularly susceptible to the modifications required for the Nemesis Program. Several dozen test subjects—all prisoners from the Raccoon City Penitentiary who had volunteered on the promise of parole if they lived (that last qualifier was left out of the original offer, of course)—had had fatal reactions to the attempted modifications.

But when Addison had been attacked by one of the lickers in the Hive, he'd responded differently than expected. The man was as good as dead anyhow, so Cain saw no good reason not to put him in the Nemesis Program and see what could be done.

As an added bonus, they had learned a great deal about the group that Addison belonged to—a misbegotten collection of wealthy liberals, bitter law-enforcement personnel, and other detritus of society who were trying to bring Umbrella down. Cain had already taken steps to make sure that Aaron Vricella and the rest of Addison's cronies were taken care of.

Meanwhile, Addison was serving to further the cause of the very corporation he was trying so misguidedly to put out of business. If Nemesis worked—and it was looking more and more like it did—then they had a super-soldier that would, Cain knew, be of great interest to his former fellows in the armed forces.

Nemesis stood eight feet tall, with muscles far larger

than those of the greatest bodybuilder. Assorted wires and pipes provided electronic and cybernetic enhancement to his already considerable strength and stamina, as well as four of his five senses (the exception being taste, which they had actually deadened, since an acute sense of taste would be an impediment to field work), and tubes fed a variety of stimulants into his bloodstream.

In one redwood-sized arm, he held a rail gun like it weighed nothing. In the other, he held the specially modified rocket launcher that few could lift even two-handed.

Now he fired that rocket launcher, even as he continued to barrage the roof of the building with the rail gun.

Moments later, the roof, the building, and Michael Guthrie all disintegrated in a fiery conflagration that did Timothy Cain's heart proud.

Nemesis then turned toward the gun shop.

TWENTY

After that fine-lookin' crazy-ass white bitch in the blue tube top shot Rashonda, L.J. had got his ass the hell *out* of the RCPD. It was safer on the street.

Though not by a whole lot, that was for goddamn sure.

The bitch had the right idea, though. L.J. might have been born and raised in Raccoon, but enough was fuckin' *enough*. No way he was keepin' his narrow ass in this town. He wanted zombies, he'd rent a fuckin' movie. Nah, dog, L.J. was going where a nigger could *live*.

L.J. got to his crib as fast as he could move his ass so he could get his Uzis and his lucky ring. He hadn't been wearin' the ring 'cause it was too fuckin' heavy when he was doin' three-card. The gold ring spelled out the word **LOVE**, 'cause L.J. was *all* about that.

He also stuck his Rick James CD in his pocket.

Never should've left the house without his guns, his ring, and his Rick.

Shit, that was probably why he was busted.

Now he just needed a ride.

Thing was, L.J.'s ride got took last month when Junior Bunk decided that L.J. wasn't allowed to be no three days late with the payments. That, and L.J. told Bunk that maybe he needed to adjust his Ritalin. Motherfucker had *no* sense of humor, and that meant that L.J.'s Chevy was at Bunk's chop shop. By now, the engine was in Baltimore, the battery in Seattle, the radiator in New York, and the body in fuckin' Japan.

But L.J. always landed on his feet, and as soon as he walked out the door, he found a beautiful red Camaro just sittin' in the middle of the street.

L.J. looked around, but didn't see nobody. When he moved closer, he could hear that it was still running. He looked in the window, and sure enough, the key was still up in there.

Well, shit, a nigger ain't gonna look no gift horse in its fuckin' mouth.

The passenger door was open, and L.J. saw some blood on the floor, but, shit, his Chevy had blood on the floor. That shit don't ever come out, and L.J. was used to that. Probably belonged to one of those zombie-ass motherfuckers.

The Camaro even had a CD player.

Just as he got into the driver's seat, some white boy fell onto the hood, scaring the *shit* out of L.J. He had the zombie eyes and those fuckin' teeth.

"Move yo' ass, motherfucker!"

He gunned the motor, threw it into drive, then slammed on the brakes.

Not only did the zombie-ass motherfucker fall off the hood, but when he hit the gas, the other door closed. Saved L.J. the fuckin' hassle.

After running over the zombie, L.J. drove on, putting the CD in the player.

All L.J. wanted was to get his ass out of Raccoon. Everywhere he turned was another zombie-ass motherfucker.

L.J. was sick and fuckin' tired of zombie-ass motherfuckers.

Then he saw a meter maid shuffling her ass down the street with her arm hangin' off her body.

Back when L.J. had the Chevy, the meter maids were always goin' up on his ass, givin' him tickets and shit. L.J. never put money in the meters—he was a paper money operation, he didn't deal in no small-change shit, so it wasn't like he carried quarters around. He had a cell phone, so it wasn't like he needed quarters for phone calls, neither.

So he veered toward the meter maid and ran her down.

"G.T.A., motherfucker! Ten points, sucker! Kiss my *entire* ass!"

Laughing, and singing along with Rick James—after all these years, Rick was still the *man*—he turned the corner onto Harbor Street.

This was the one street he was gonna miss when he

got his ass outta town. The Playa's Club was here. Many a late night he'd spent putting singles in some big-titted bitch's G-string, giving them twenties for table dances, and sometimes, if he was lucky and had enough big bills, getting to take one in the back alley.

His favorite was LaWanda. That girl could *move*—a booty that would not quit, and the best tits money could buy.

And there she was now, stumbling down the street on her platforms, wearing a white tank top and black leather miniskirt, and with a big-ass hole in her leg.

On the one hand, L.J. was sorry she was dead. On the other hand, she still looked *damn* fine.

"Shit, bitch," he called out to the zombie ho, "you still got it!"

She wasn't wearing a bra under the white tank top. L.J. decided that, zombie-ass bitch or no zombie-ass bitch, she was still one *fine* piece of ass.

Then an airbag exploded in his face, right when he felt a sharp pain in his back.

It took him a few minutes to get his head on straight, but finally he got his ass out from under the fuckin' airbag and tried to open the door.

It wouldn't budge.

He shouldered the fuckin' thing, and then it screeched open like fingernails on a fuckin' chalkboard. He fell out of the car, and saw that the Camaro was trashed, mostly because L.J. had been so busy checkin' out the booty on the ho that he didn't see the booty of the abandoned Ford in the middle of the street.

The Camaro was totaled. Besides, L.J. wasn't drivin' around with no airbag flappin' out. That shit was *weak*.

As he got to his feet, he found himself surrounded by zombie-ass motherfuckers: the meter maid, the ho, and a whole bunch of other people.

"Oh, shit."

He ran.

One good thing about zombie-ass motherfuckers was that they couldn't run for shit, so L.J. had no problem making it to the intersection of Harbor and Main.

He turned onto Main to find more zombie-ass motherfuckers walkin' down the street.

"Damn, dog, you in a motherfuckin' Michael Jackson video."

One building still had lights on and signs of life. *Real* life. Mostly Colt. L.J. knew the place—some brothers got their hardware here, but not L.J. The guy who ran it was a redneck white boy named Lance Halloran. L.J. didn't buy his heat from no white folks.

Today, though, was no time to be fuckin' choosy.

He ran in just as someone was trying to close the door.

"Hold up," he cried, "hold up!"

Just as he squeezed through the door, he looked around.

Cops.

A whole room full of cops.

Worse, they were all S.T.A.R.S.

"Shee-it!"

The only two of these white folks not wearing fuckin'

S.T.A.R.S. gear were Halloran and another old white motherfucker wearin' a tie. He had to be a cop, too.

"Maybe I was safer out there—this all looks like some white supremacist bullshit."

They all looked at him like he was fuckin' crazy.

Well, at this point, L.J. *was* fuckin' crazy. Especially since it looked like he was holin' up with these white folks.

"You know you ain't inheritin' the earth, mother-fuckers, right?"

The plainclothes cop was holding a pump-action shotgun. He held it up—L.J. flinched, but then he handed it *to* L.J.

"Here."

A white motherfucker giving a Negro a shotgun. Mark this day down on the fuckin' calendar, dog!

But he didn't need no white-folks charity. He held open his coat to show off his Uzis.

"Nigger, *please*—my shit is *custom.*"

"Damn right, L.J.," Halloran said. "I don't sell that shit here."

"Yeah, Halloran, you just sell to cracker-ass white folks who blow up fuckin' Bambi with shotguns and shit."

The cop turned to Halloran. "You know this asshole, Lance?"

"L.J. Wayne. He's the usual street garbage."

Holding up one of his Uzis, L.J. said, "Watch yo' mouth, Halloran. I'm fuckin' exceptional street garbage, and you know why?"

"Why?" The cop was actually laughing now.

"'Cause I'm still breathin' and not no zombie-ass motherfucker, that's why."

"Damn right," the cop said. "I'm Captain Henderson. You want to stay here, you do what I tell you when I tell you to do it, or I'll shoot you myself. Clear?"

"As fuckin' mud, *Captain.* Let's blow up some zombie shit."

Henderson smiled, then turned back to Halloran. "Let's get those shutters down."

"No problem," Halloran said, giving L.J. a look. "I'll be right there."

Just as Halloran got over to the front window and reached for the handle to start pulling the metal shutters down, L.J. said, "What the *fuck* is that?"

L.J.'d seen a lotta shit in his life—he'd seen a lotta shit *today*—but he'd never seen *nothin'* like this.

A white dude who was *at least* nine fuckin' feet tall. Tubes and shit goin' in and out of his hands, muscles to make Arnold fuckin' Schwarzeneggar look like Arnold fuckin' Palmer.

This wasn't no zombie.

This was worse.

And L.J. didn't think it could get no worse than zombies.

The big dude was holding two big-ass pieces of hardware. The first was one of those guns they had on helicopters—except this motherfucker was *holding* it.

In his other hand was a rocket launcher.

L.J. was thinkin' he should've retrieved the Rick

James CD from the wrecked Camaro. He needed all the luck he could get right now.

Then the big dude started *shooting* the rail gun at one of the buildings next door.

"Shit, that's where Guthrie is!" one of the cops yelled.

Henderson shot that cop a look that almost scared L.J. more than he was already scared. "What the *fuck* is Guthrie doing there?"

The cop shrugged. "Said he wanted to practice his shooting."

Before Henderson could start talkin' shit about this Guthrie asshole, the big dude hefted the rocket launcher and blew up the building he was shooting at.

Looking at Halloran, who was takin' his sweet fuckin' time with the shutters, Henderson yelled, "Hurry it up!"

L.J. was still in shock. "Holy shit—*look* at that big motherfucker."

The last shutter came crashing down like those gates on those old fuckin' castles they had in Europe and shit.

"No way that son of a bitch is getting in here," Halloran said.

What, were these cops all fuckin' stupid? "He got himself a rocket launcher, dog! We 'bout to explode up in here!"

"Take cover, dammit!" Henderson yelled.

All the cops took up positions behind displays and counters.

L.J. realized he was standing alone in the middle of

the store, and he did *not* like that. He ran behind the counter where Henderson was. When in doubt, stay with the motherfucker in charge.

The sound that came next was so fuckin' loud L.J. had to drop his Uzis in order to cover his ears. The big dude was using the helicopter gun on the front of the store.

Then silence. L.J.'s ears were still ringing—shit, they'd probably be ringing for an hour—but the big dude was done shooting.

Now there was a big-ass hole in the front, just about the size of the big dude. It was like when some cartoon character went through a fuckin' wall and the hole was shaped just like the character.

L.J. picked up his Uzi and aimed it at the door. No motherfuckin' big white dude with a rocket launcher was gettin' the drop on L.J. Wayne, no *fuckin'* way!

He waited.

And waited.

And waited.

Where the fuck *was* that thing?

Then he heard a big fuckin' crash, and he started coughing.

The big dude came *through the fuckin' ceiling,* and L.J. was eating fuckin' plaster dust. The dude started firing the helicopter gun, even as the cops returned fire.

L.J. just sat behind the counter, frozen like a fuckin' ice cream cone. No fuckin' way he was movin'. He was too busy praying, and hoping hell wouldn't be as bad as Momma always said it would be.

KEITH R.A. DeCANDIDO

One of the cops came running in from the back. He had an MP5K, and he fired it on full fuckin' automatic.

The big dude didn't even fuckin' *flinch*. He just swung around and fired the rail gun right at the cop.

L.J. looked to his right and saw that Henderson had more holes in him than fuckin' Swiss cheese. He looked around and saw that the other cops were dead, too.

Sheeeeeeee-it!

The only other person in Mostly Colt still alive besides L.J. and the big dude was Halloran.

He stood up from behind the counter with his shotgun.

And did that white motherfucker look *pissed!*

"Fuck you!" he screamed as he pumped his shotgun and fired it right into the big dude's stomach.

Nothin'. The big dude didn't even really react. Just nothin'.

Until he raised up the helicopter gun and fired on Halloran.

L.J. was nobody's bitch, and he sure as shit knew better than to pull a gun on a ten-foot-tall motherfucker who'd just killed a room full of cops.

He dropped his Uzis.

"Respect," he said quickly, and closed his eyes, waiting for the big dude to blow his black ass to hell. "Peace, dog—peace."

The only thing L.J. was sorry about was that he'd never apologized to Momma for getting her involved in that pyramid scheme. Took her *years* to pay off the fine, too. He'd have helped, but he had his own problems.

After several seconds, L.J. still wasn't dead.

He opened his eyes.

The big dude was walking out of the shop through the big-ass cartoon character hole in the shutters.

Sheeeee-it.

Maybe wearing the ring was enough good luck.

✝WEN✝Y-ONE

Jill Valentine watched as the woman named Alice stripped down her weaponry.

At first glance, Alice wasn't anything great to look at. Oh, sure, she had a supermodel's good looks, but she had an ordinary physique—in decent shape, but she didn't look any more or less fit than any other civilian who worked out every day.

But what Jill had seen today wasn't human.

Then again, Raccoon City seemed to be overrun with things that weren't human tonight.

After taking the mystery phone call, Alice had led Jill, Peyton, and Morales to an abandoned streetcar in an alley off Swann Road to fill them in on what she'd learned. Jill managed to keep her exterior cool despite what was going on, mainly because *someone* had to. Peyton was fighting a losing battle with unconsciousness, and Morales was a goddamn basket case.

The field-stripping was being done unconsciously while Alice spoke. If this kept up, Jill was going to start getting a serious inferiority complex.

"His name," Alice said, "is Dr. Charles Ashford. He runs the Advanced Genetics and Viral Research Division of Umbrella."

Morales blinked. "He works for *them?*"

"That's right."

"What's he want with us?" Jill asked. That this Ashford person worked for Umbrella was self-evident—there was no way he could tap into the RCPD traffic cameras otherwise. One would think that as a reporter—well, ex-reporter—Morales would know what questions were relevant and which ones were stupid.

Then again, she was an *ex*-reporter.

Alice answered Jill's query. "His daughter Angela is trapped within the city. We find her, and he'll help us escape the perimeter."

"No deal," Peyton said in a ragged voice. "I say we find the building with the thickest walls and the strongest doors and we barricade ourselves in. Sit tight and wait for help."

Jill shook her head. Under other circumstances, she'd agree with her boss's plan. But she had the feeling that it wouldn't be that easy.

Alice confirmed that feeling. "There won't be any help. According to Ashford, Umbrella knows it can't contain the infection. So at sunrise, Raccoon City will be completely sanitized."

Morales went pale. "Sanitized?"

"A precision tactical nuclear device—a half-megaton yield. It'll destroy the infection and all evidence of it."

Despite expecting an answer along those lines, Jill shuddered. Morales looked stunned. Peyton looked as shocked as he could, given his pasty white complexion and the way he was sweating.

"I don't believe it," Peyton said. "I mean, how would they get away with this? It'd be all over the news."

"The cover story is already being prepared—that's the only reason why they're waiting until morning. A meltdown at the nuclear power plant—a tragic accident."

Peyton shook his head. "Not even Umbrella is capable of this."

Jill thought back to her own situation. Umbrella had made an entire forest-full of zombies disappear and managed to turn cop against cop by convincing the RCPD brass to toss one of their best officers—her—to the wolves. They also were capable of creating this situation in the first place.

Why not wipe out an entire city?

She turned to Alice. "You know these people—what do you think?"

Without hesitating, Alice said, "I think we should be out of here by sunrise."

As if to accentuate her point, she clicked the ammo clip into one of her Uzis.

"Fine," Jill said, "then let's get a move on." She had already reloaded both her automatics and holstered them. She helped Peyton to his feet. "Where do we go?"

"Ashford said his daughter is hiding out in her school—it's the one on Hudson and Robertson."

"How can he be so sure?"

"The city's covered in surveillance cameras. He has access to them."

"Great. That doesn't mean we should trust him."

"We don't have to."

Jill shook her head. The whole situation sucked, but that had been true all day. At least now they were *doing* something.

Besides, Jill didn't like the idea of a little girl trapped in this hellhole. Even if her father was a higher-up at Umbrella.

"What if there is no way out of the city?" she asked Alice as they disembarked from the streetcar into the back end of the alley.

Alice shrugged. "You had other plans for tonight?"

Jill grinned wryly. "Nah, I always dress like this."

When Alice returned the smile—a full-blown one, not the smirk she'd employed periodically—Jill realized that it was the first time she'd seen the woman make that particular facial expression. She still had that hard-edged look—like a Japanese *katana*, elegant yet indestructible—but the smile made her look slightly more human.

Then the smile fell and Alice stopped walking.

"Wait."

They were still in the alley, right next to an abandoned RCPD squad car. Alice looked down the alley at something at the mouth that emptied onto Swann.

"What is it?" Jill asked.

But Alice just kept staring down the alley.

Peyton started to walk past Alice, but she put a hand on his arm.

"No."

Glowering down at the unwelcome hand, Peyton almost growled, "Sunrise isn't going to wait."

"There's something out there." Alice spoke with a surety and finality that worried Jill.

Jill didn't see anything—no movement, nothing. Part of her wanted to believe Alice was telling the truth, but she didn't really know a damn thing about this woman.

On the other hand, Alice had already demonstrated that she could've killed all three of them several times over, and hadn't—a mercy she hadn't extended to the monsters in the church or the zombies in the cemetery. That was at the very least a basis for *some* kind of trust.

But Jill still didn't see a goddamn thing at the end of the alley except for the end of the alley.

"I don't see anything," Peyton said irritably.

"That doesn't alter the fact that there's something out there." Again, the surety in Alice's tone.

"We don't have *time* for this bullshit." Peyton pushed past Alice and proceeded down the alley.

"No—" Alice started, but Peyton ignored her.

Jill was about to join him when the report of dozens of rounds being fired at once slammed into her ears—

—just as the cause of those reports slammed into

Peyton's form. Blood splattered as the bullets tore through his body, and he went flying backward.

He was dead before he hit the ground, which he did about six feet behind where he was standing.

"Peyton! No!"

Jill looked up as a figure stepped out of the shadows.

"Figure" was truly an inadequate word. The person was eight feet tall at least, with huge muscles, and tubes running in and out of his flesh; he was carrying a big weapon that was roughly the size of Texas, and wearing a rocket launcher slung across his back in the exact same way Alice had her shotgun slung across *her* back.

How the hell this guy had managed to hide in the shadows was beyond Jill's understanding.

Morales looked like she had shit in her socks. "What *is* that? Someone tell me, what the hell *is* that?"

"Nemesis."

Jill whirled toward Alice, who had whispered that word.

Then she looked down at the corpse of Peyton Wells.

Unlike the higher-ups in the RCPD, Peyton had always believed Jill—more to the point, he'd believed *in* Jill. Not everyone was a hundred percent thrilled with a good-looking young woman in S.T.A.R.S. The facts that she was a crack shot and a brilliant officer, and had saved the mayor's life, were secondary to the fact that she was a good-looking young woman, and therefore couldn't *possibly* be good enough for S.T.A.R.S. unless she'd fucked her way to the top. Peyton had taken on anyone who'd tried to accuse her of that—not that she needed the help, she defended herself just fine against the sexist assholes, but she still appreciated the support.

Peyton had even chewed out Henderson when Jill was suspended, almost earning a suspension of his own.

Now he lay dead in an alley.

Jill Valentine had seen a lot of corpses today, more than she'd seen even in a lifetime of law enforcement.

But of all the bodies she'd seen today, this was the first one she cared about.

The next thing she knew, she was charging this Nemesis thing with both automatics blazing.

Every shot struck its target.

For all the good it did.

Nemesis didn't even flinch at the shots she threw.

He did, however, raise the arm holding the big gun.

As Jill dived behind a garbage skip, automatics still blazing, she finally recognized Nemesis's "handgun" as a rail gun. If even one bullet connected, it'd rip through her body like tissue paper.

Just like they had Peyton.

Both automatics clicked empty as she landed behind the skip. The staccato report of the rail gun matched time with the bullets hitting the skip a millisecond later, but none of the bullets penetrated.

Yet.

Jill reloaded and wondered how they were going to get out of this. Every single one of her shots had hit— Jill had never missed before, and she hadn't missed now.

But this Nemesis thing was apparently bulletproof.

Just fucking great.

Then the firing stopped.

Jill risked looking up over the skip.

She saw Nemesis staring at Alice.

And Alice staring at Nemesis.

Behind them, Morales was filming the whole thing. More fodder for her goddamn Emmy.

What the fuck was going on *now?*

"You have to leave," Alice said to Jill without looking at her. She and Nemesis were in a classic staredown. "Now!"

Involuntarily, Jill looked down at Peyton's body.

Even though she never stopped staring at Nemesis, somehow Alice knew Jill was looking at her friend. "He's dead. You can join him—or you can do as I say."

Jill was still looking at Peyton's body.

Whatever else one could say, he was definitely dead. He had more holes in him than Julius Caesar.

For whatever insane reason, she trusted Alice. For whatever insane reason, Alice was taking on Nemesis alone.

They were fucking welcome to each other.

Jill ran out of the alley. The first thing she saw was a pickup truck that was sitting in the middle of Swann Road at a right angle to the double yellow line. The driver's-side door was wide open. Jill clambered under the dash and started prying open the ignition panel so she could hot-wire it.

To Jill's surprise, Morales climbed in on the passenger side.

"What," Jill asked without looking at the reporter, "you're not gonna film the big fight?"

"The hell with that—I want out of here. That Ashford guy wants us to find his daughter so we can leave, I'll take that deal. I'm not winding up like your friend Wells."

Jill ground her teeth but said nothing as she continued her efforts.

"Besides—she's insane. She can't take that thing."

The engine roared to life. Jill mentally thanked her father for all the skills he'd taught her during a misspent youth, and started to extricate herself from the truck—

—only to find herself face to face with the bloody, bullet-ridden form of Peyton Wells.

"Peyton!"

The parts of his face that weren't covered in blood were even paler, and his eyes were watery.

Jill unholstered one of her automatics, even as Peyton tried to bite her on the neck.

She kicked him away and aimed the gun at his head.

But she couldn't pull the trigger.

Then Peyton lunged again.

Morales screamed.

Jill's own words to Alice in the graveyard came back to her: *If it comes to that—I'll take care of it myself.*

She squeezed the trigger.

Peyton's head snapped back upon the bullet's impact. Then his now-completely-dead form fell forward into Jill's arms.

Revulsed, Jill jumped back into the cab of the pickup, letting Peyton's body fall to the ground.

"Jesus goddamn shit-sucking Christ."

"Amen," Morales muttered.

"C'mon," Jill said, "we've got a little kid to rescue."

She closed the door, put on her seat belt, threw the truck into gear, and started straight down Swann.

Then a figure leapt in front of the truck.

TWENTY-TWO

Alice stared at Nemesis.

She knew about the Nemesis Program, of course—as head of security for the Hive, she *had* to know about it.

But, as far as she was aware, the project hadn't been going well. All the previous attempts to create a super-weapon had failed miserably.

Yet here she was, face to face with a success.

A fucking tall one, too.

Alice cursed herself for taking things too slowly. She had gotten the idea to use Lisa Broward to help expose Umbrella for the bastards they were weeks ago, but she had proceeded cautiously. First she'd had to make sure that Lisa was the right person for the job.

Then she had to recruit her, which she did over lunch at Che Buono.

So what happened? The very *day* that she pulled the trigger on the plan was the same day that Spence decided to unleash the T-virus on the Hive as a cover for his stealing it.

If she had done it even a day sooner, none of this would have happened.

She continued to stare at Nemesis.

Something seemed familiar about his eyes.

No, it was more than that—there was something familiar about *Nemesis*. Not just the body, but the very concept, as bizarre as that seemed.

Her heart beat loudly in her chest. Since she'd awakened in the Raccoon City Hospital, her heightened senses had made her aware of her heartbeat, but this was even more intense than before.

After a moment, she realized why.

She wasn't hearing just her own heart—she also heard Nemesis's.

And it was in perfect time with her own.

Then Nemesis took a step forward.

So did Alice.

She drew both her Uzis.

Nemesis lifted the rail gun.

Alice fired both Uzis into Nemesis.

The creature didn't even slow down as the bullets slammed into his chest.

They charged each other like two bulls going at it, right up until they were three steps from colliding.

Then Alice leapt into the air, flipping up and over Nemesis's eight-foot-tall frame and landing solidly behind him.

Before Nemesis could turn to face her, she ran toward the basketball court that was behind the alley.

She slammed the gate behind her as she ran into the court, but that, predictably, didn't slow Nemesis down. However, to Alice's surprise, Nemesis didn't just tear through the chain-link fence.

He stepped on the RCPD squad car and then jumped over the fence.

When Nemesis landed on the court, he cracked the pavement beneath his massive feet. Then he raised one huge fist, and brought it down.

Had Alice not rolled and tumbled out of the way, that fist would have pulped her entire body.

She kept moving, never giving Nemesis a chance to get a bead on her, dashing about the basketball court. Unfortunately, being in an enclosed area didn't help matters. Her biggest advantage was speed and agility, and she needed space for that.

Within moments, he had her trapped in a corner.

So she ran up the fence and dived over the top, landing gracefully on her feet on the other side.

That would, she knew, give her only a few seconds' head start.

If she was lucky, it would be enough.

She ran out onto Swann Road, crossing the street to an office building at the corner of Cleveland Street. The door was actually around the corner on Cleveland, but there was a perfectly good window right in front of her.

Alice ran, leapt, and dived through the window, covering her face with her arms.

Just as she did, she heard the report of the rail gun. Fuck.

Cold pain sliced through her arms and shoulders as shards of glass cut into her skin, followed immediately by a single hot pain in her left arm.

One of the rail gun's bullets had hit her.

The amazing thing was that only one shot had connected.

Rolling across the floor, now littered with broken glass, Alice tumbled into an upright position and started running away, ignoring the blood and the pain.

Behind her came the booming sound of eight feet of genetically engineered monstrosity walking through a wall and shattering the plaster and brick.

Alice hoped like hell he didn't come through a support beam.

The one way in which Alice's speed didn't help her was in a chase, by virtue of Nemesis having considerably longer strides. The monster was already closing the distance, so Alice just ran ahead without thought to where she was going.

This turned out to be a mistake. Within seconds, she found herself facing a dead end, with only a wall containing a mail chute covered by a metal door in front of her, and no other way out except backward.

But backward was Nemesis with his two oversize weapons.

Without breaking stride, she raised her Uzis and started firing on the mail chute door, then dived for it headfirst as she'd done through the window moments earlier, gambling that her enhanced strength and the bullet power would weaken the chute door enough for her to penetrate it.

Luckily, the gamble paid off. She smashed through the door, pain ripping into her bones from the impact, and tumbled down the chute.

The very thin chute. No way that Nemesis could fit down here, nor did the structure allow the possibility of his opening the space up further. The only way he could follow her would be to go outside and around to the back of the building.

She landed on the floor of the basement in a heap. Ten feet to her right was the oversize mail bin that normally sat under the chute—and which she had been hoping would break her fall—tipped over and ripped to pieces.

As she clambered to her feet, several white-hot lances of pain sliced through her left arm. She had dislocated her shoulder coming through the chute door, been shot in the biceps, and broken two of her fingers when she landed. Not to mention all the cuts from the glass.

After running across the room, she slumped against a wall, on the far end from the room's only entrance, and behind several more mail bins. With any luck, Nemesis wouldn't see her when he came in the door.

One-handed, she fashioned a tourniquet from a strip

of canvas torn from one of the damaged mail bins and used it to stop the bleeding of her gunshot wound.

Years ago, when she was still with the Treasury Department, Alice had been involved in a fight with a mugger who mistook her for a helpless young woman walking down a dark Washington, D.C., street. She'd disabused him of that notion in fairly short order, but not before the punk sliced open her left shoulder with his switchblade.

Alice still carried the scar from that encounter, but more important, she remembered the searing agony of that knife wound when it was first inflicted, and the continuing pain as it slowly healed. It was weeks before she had full use of her left arm again—maddening, since Alice was, in fact, left-handed.

What struck her now was that the trauma she'd suffered today was several orders of magnitude worse than that knife wound—yet the pain was nowhere near as debilitating.

Intellectually, she knew she should have fainted from the shock, or from the blood loss.

She did neither.

Instead, she shoved her shoulder and her broken finger bones back into their sockets.

The pain was beyond tremendous, yet Alice felt it only on an intellectual level. It wasn't debilitating.

She added this to the ledger of Things Umbrella Had Done to Her.

Looking down at her arm, she saw that the cuts from the broken glass had already healed.

Satisfied that she'd be able to keep going, she got to her feet. Her right leg, which was feeling wonky after her landing in the basement, now felt fine.

Still no sign of Nemesis.

So she risked heading toward the only door. They still had a little girl to rescue.

Twenty-Three

All Jill Valentine wanted to do was get out of Raccoon City.

If she was brutally honest with herself—and what better time than now as she drove a hot-wired truck through the dead streets of the city alongside a frightened weathergirl shortly after having shot one of her best friends in the head after he was turned into a zombie?—that had been her goal since they first suspended her.

All she had ever cared about was becoming an RCPD cop. The biggest thrill of her life had been when she graduated the academy, matched only by the tremendous honor of being tapped for S.T.A.R.S.

But now the city had gone crazy and was dying. No, scratch that, it was dead. It had died the moment Um-

KEITH R.A. DeCandido

brella started doing zombie experiments. That had led both to Jill's suspension—irreparably damaging her career as a cop in this town—and to today's disaster.

Her entire life had been reduced to one imperative: get out of Raccoon.

Right now, that meant finding Angela Ashford so her father would clear their way out. And if the father tried to renege on the deal, Jill had no problem with using Angela as a hostage to get what she wanted.

That might not quite be by the good-guy playbook, but Jill was beyond caring at this point.

She looked down briefly at her hands. They were still covered in blood.

Peyton's blood.

When she looked up, she saw a man jumping up and down in front of her in the middle of the road.

Instinctively, Jill hit the brakes. Something was familiar about this guy.

Then she remembered—the perp who'd almost been bitten by the zombie hooker in the squad room.

He was already talking a mile a minute, just as he had in the squad room, and he had no obvious wounds, so he hadn't been infected.

Yet.

The perp ran to the driver's-side window, only to find the muzzle of one of Jill's automatics in his face.

Holding up his hands, the perp cried, "It's cool, Officer, it's cool! I ain't one 'a them things! Ain't even bit."

To prove his point, he did a full three-sixty. His

clothes were a bit scuffed, and ugly as all hell, but he was definitely not seriously injured.

Indicating the passenger side with her head, she said, "Climb aboard."

As the perp walked around to the other side of the truck, he said, "Damn—I thought I was the last man alive, but when I heard the shooting, I came runnin'."

He opened the door and slid in beside Morales, offering her his hand.

"Lloyd Jefferson Wayne. You can call me L.J. on account of the informal situation."

Before L.J. could even close the door, Jill put the truck back into drive and proceeded down the street.

"Terri Morales." She shook L.J.'s hand.

L.J. almost leapt out of the seat. "Shit, I know you! I *know* you! You do the weather—you're a goddamn celebrity!"

"Yes, that's me," Morales said, brightening for the first time since Ravens' Gate.

Jill ground her teeth. She'd lost Peyton, Alice was off playing footsie with the Frankenstein monster, and who was she stuck with? A starstruck small-time punk and the Raccoon 7 weather chick.

The option of shooting herself in the head was looking more and more palatable.

"This is the *shit!* Terri fuckin' Morales, you da bomb, girl!"

"Well, thank you, L.J., it's nice to be appreciated."

On the other hand, Jill liked the idea of shooting Morales and L.J. in the head a lot more.

As she turned the pickup onto Hudson Avenue, L.J. said, "Yo, cop lady, where the fuck we goin'? 'Cause I'm tellin' you right now, this ain't the way outta town, and there ain't nowhere else to be but gone, you know what I'm sayin'?"

"'We' are going to find a little girl named Angela Ashford."

"You shittin' me. We supposed to find one little kid in this town? We talkin' needles and haystacks, yo."

"We know where she probably is," Jill said. "When we find her, her father's going to get us out of town."

"Yeah, okay, I'm all for that. I seen shit today that would turn me white. If you can get me outta here and someplace where they don't have zombie-ass mother-fuckers and big-ass white folks with tubes in they arms that shoot up cops—"

"What did you say?" Jill asked quickly.

"What did I say what?"

"Who shot up cops?"

"This twelve-foot-tall motherfucker with tubes and packin' *mad* heat shot up Mostly Colt. Some cop named Henderson and a bunch of them moon units."

Jill gripped the steering wheel tighter. "You mean S.T.A.R.S."

"What-the-fuck-ever, bitch, point is, they all dead now thanks to that big-ass dude. So faster you can get my narrow ass outta here, the happier I'll be."

"Understand something, asshole," Jill said tightly. "You help out, you get out of town, too. Get even a little in my way—or get bit by one of our fellow townspeople—and I will put a bullet in that pea you call a brain, understand?"

L.J. held up his hands. "Hey, it's cool, yo, it's cool. You the boss-lady."

"Just remember that."

As she drove the pickup through the intersection of Hudson and Robertson, Jill shook her head.

Henderson was dead. She supposed that was some kind of karmic payback for Peyton buying it.

She wondered who else had been with Henderson. Probably Markinson—if he ever got too far from Henderson's ass, his nose would suffer withdrawal symptoms—and maybe Wyrnowski. And if they were at a gun shop, that redneck Guthrie was almost guaranteed to be with them, too.

All dead.

Latest in a series, collect 'em all.

It wasn't hard for Jill to make out the school—of all the buildings on this part of Hudson, it was the only one that still had its lights on.

Jill wondered if that was a good sign or not.

She parked the car just outside the school gates. Nearby, she sighted a vehicle crashed into one of the buildings by the abandoned playground. From this distance, it looked like an RCPD truck, but she couldn't tell which division—and she didn't care enough at this point to investigate.

They had a girl to find.

Meanwhile, L.J. had gone back to stargazing. "Terri fuckin' Morales. So, is it hard? To get on TV and shit?"

"It just takes a lot of hard work and determination," Morales said with a bright smile that Jill had to resist the urge to punch.

Both weapons drawn, Jill approached the front door to the school. Morales and L.J. were right behind her.

The door was ajar. It squeaked as Jill pushed it open.

"Damn, we got some serious horror-movie shit happenin' here." L.J. had gone fully three seconds without talking, which was obviously more than he could bear.

Ahead of them was a long, darkened corridor filled with lockers and doors to classrooms.

Morales muttered, "I always hated school."

"Not me." L.J. shrugged. "I was my school's ghetto superstar. Guns, drugs, hos, jazz choice—I did it renaissance style!"

Jill had finally had it. "Is there any danger you might shut the fuck up for a moment?"

L.J. held up his hands defensively but, miraculously, said nothing.

"We're going to have to split up to cover this place."

"Forget it," Morales said. "I don't even have a gun. I'm not going anywhere by myself."

"I could come with you," L.J. said quickly, flashing a huge smile.

Looking at L.J., Jill said, "You take the east wing." Then she handed one of her pistols to Morales. "You take the west."

Morales took the automatic, holding it like it was a dead rat.

"I've never shot a gun before."

Resisting the urge to say that if she shot herself in the foot, she'd be doing them all a favor, Jill instead put on an encouraging voice. "Nothing to it. Point, pull, repeat." With a smile, she added, "Try to hit them in the head."

Under normal circumstances, Jill wouldn't split them up this way, given that L.J. was at best unreliable and Morales at best wholly incompetent, but time *was* of the essence. If they weren't out of Raccoon by sunrise, their continued good fortune in managing to stay alive in the death trap that the city had become would come to an abrupt end.

They needed to find Angela Ashford, and fast.

Jill took the basement, figuring that to be the most likely spot where she'd be. After all, if a little kid was hiding out, she'd go downstairs.

As she opened the door to the basement, she heard Morales mutter to herself, "Point, pull, repeat, point, pull, repeat, point, pull, repeat . . ."

If she was really lucky, Jill would find the kid and be able to get out before L.J. and Morales knew she was gone.

No, that wasn't fair. They deserved as much of a chance to live—

—as Peyton had?

Dammit.

The basement was a maze of cooling ducts, heating pipes, and bad lighting. Jill had a flashlight, but it barely penetrated the gloom.

Anything could be hiding down here.

ᛏWEᏁᛏY-FOUR

Humming the theme to *Shaft*—he'd have been singing it, but aside from the phrase "shut yo' mouth!" he couldn't remember any of the words—L.J. walked through the halls of the darkened school.

This, he decided, was cool. Yeah, okay, most everyone in the town was dead, but L.J. was still kickin', and that was what mattered. And now he was patrollin' the halls on a mission to rescue a little girl.

All this after surviving the fuckin' St. Valentine's Day Massacre in Halloran's gun shop.

Best of all, he was hangin' with Terri fuckin' Morales! A goddamn celebrity!

Not bad for a three-time loser from the 'hood.

He went into the first room he came across in this wing. Looked like a science lab—it had those big blacktopped tables with faucets and Bunsen burners and shit. Against the wall, there were all kinds of jars filled with dirty water and dead animals.

L.J. shook his head. No wonder the world was goin' crazy, if they were lettin' little kids play with this shit.

On the far side of the room was a frosted-glass door. Probably where the teacher kept all the spare bodies and shit. Jesus.

Then he blinked—he saw something in the damn window!

Sheeee-it.

L.J.'s first instinct was to get his ass out of there, but then he stopped.

He'd survived the cop house being turned into *Night of the Living Dead*.

He'd survived almost getting eaten by Rashonda-the-zombie-ass-ho.

He'd survived a car crash.

And best of all, he'd survived the big-ass mother-fucker shooting up a room full of cops.

So he could survive this shit, no problem.

He walked up to the door.

Put his hand on the handle.

Took his hand off the handle.

Resisted the urge to run away again.

Finally yanked opened the door, raising his custom Uzi, ready to bust a cap *right* in that zombie's ass!

On the other side of the door was a skeleton. One of those jive-ass plastic skeletons hanging from a hook like the ones L.J. used to dress up in pimp outfits when he was in school.

Sheeee-it.

L.J. was pissed off and glad at the same time. Yeah, sure, he didn't have to face off against one of those zombie-ass motherfuckers—on the other hand, he didn't *get* to face off against one of those zombie-ass motherfuckers, he just got to look like an asshole.

At least Terri didn't see him be no fool.

Lowering his Uzi, he turned around—

—and bumped right into a zombie-ass motherfucker!

He tried to raise his Uzi again. The zombie was a white dude with a *nasty* rug on his head and a butt-fuckin'-ugly moustache—probably a teacher, based on how the motherfucker was dressed—and he grabbed L.J.'s Uzi before he could do shit with it.

Then the zombie teacher went to bite L.J. just like Rashonda had. L.J. was trapped by the skeleton on one side and the zombie on the other.

For the second time today—shit, for the second time in his *life*—L.J. prayed.

Somebody grabbed the zombie from behind and snapped its neck.

It fell to the floor.

L.J. blinked. Some spic in a black uniform had just killed the zombie! Hot shit!

The uniform had a name tag that read **OLIVERA.**

Olivera bent over, picked up L.J.'s Uzi, and held it out.

"I think this belongs to you."

Stunned, L.J. took the gun. He also got a good look at this Olivera dude, and he looked like pure Grade-A USDA-approved shit. He was sweating like a motherfucker, and his eyes were all bloodshot. Looked like Rondell did after he got busted and went through the d.t.'s.

"You got the call as well?" Olivera asked.

"What?"

"You're here for the girl?"

L.J. nodded. "Yeah, yeah—we be lookin' for the Ashford girl. Gonna get us outta here."

"Ashford didn't say he'd made a deal with anyone else. But I guess we're partners."

"Whoa!" L.J. didn't like the sound of that. He was a *bad* mother all on his own, he didn't need no help. "Easy on the partners shit!"

Olivera stared at him.

Rondell never could stare at nobody like that when he had the d.t.'s. Shit, if the RCPD detectives could stare like that, they'd get more confessions.

L.J. said, "A'right, fine. Partners. Listen, just don't tell anyone about the gun, okay?"

"My lips are sealed," Olivera said. "Let's go."

TWENTY-FIVE

"Point, pull, repeat."

This was all D.J. McInerney's fault.

"Point, pull, repeat."

It was D.J. who'd supplied Terri Morales with the footage of Councilman Miller. It was D.J. who'd assured her that it was authentic. It was D.J. who'd told her that corroboration wasn't necessary.

"Point, pull, repeat."

If he hadn't pulled that crap on Terri, she'd still be doing the news. Hell, she'd probably have moved on to a *real* city instead of this backwater dump, doing investigative reporting somewhere interesting like Baltimore or San Francisco or Dallas. Maybe even New York or Chicago.

"Point, pull, repeat."

Or L.A.

"Point, pull, repeat."

That was her real dream, of course. Los Angeles, city of lights.

"Point, pull, repeat."

Or was that Paris?

Whatever, if it hadn't been for D.J.'s trick, she'd be in a real city reporting news right now instead of wandering the halls of an abandoned school in a city full of zombies looking for a little kid while saying "Point, pull, repeat" like it was some kind of holy mantra.

And carrying a gun.

Terri *hated* guns.

Maybe she wouldn't have to fire it.

She opened the door to one of the classrooms.

The place was a mess. Desks were overturned, papers and books were all over the floor.

Pretty much like the rest of the city.

Dutifully, she filmed the room with her camera, which felt a helluva lot more comfortable in her right hand than the stupid gun Officer Valentine had given her did in her left.

What the hell was the woman thinking, giving her a gun? It was nuts.

Sure, she'd complained that she didn't have a gun, but that was because she wanted an armed escort. She left the violence to thugs like Valentine. That's what they were *paid* for.

Terri was paid to report the news.

Or the weather.

Thanks to D.J., that bastard.

What especially pissed her off was that D.J. didn't *need* to fake the footage. Miller was dirty, everyone knew it, it was just a question of when he'd fuck up enough to get caught. In fact, he did get caught the very next week—by a goddamn *newspaper* reporter. If some ink jockey could nail Miller, anybody could. Certainly Terri could've, given a decent source.

Her mistake was in thinking that D.J. was one.

D.J. had disappeared right after the tape was exposed as an expert bit of digital fakery. That annoyed Terri for two reasons. One, she wanted to remonstrate with the little shit for ruining her career.

Two, he probably wasn't in town right now, so he'd escaped the fate of most of Raccoon City's citizenry. If anybody deserved to be turned into a zombie and shot in the head, it was D.J. McInerney.

However, she knew she'd climb out of this hole eventually. She was still famous, after all. Even street punks like L.J. knew who she was. And weather could still lead to a decent career—look at Al Roker.

She started when she heard something.

It sounded like a whimper of some sort.

"Angela?"

Moving toward the sound, Terri found a little girl cowering in the corner. It looked like she was cradling a doll in her arms.

The poor kid.

"It's okay, honey. No need to be afraid. We're here to take you home."

Terri realized that she had no idea what Angela Ashford looked like. For all she knew, this was some other little girl.

Still, even if it wasn't Ashford's daughter, it was better to rescue her than not.

The girl's back was to Terri. Setting the camera down for a moment—it wouldn't be a good idea to put the gun down with little kids about—she touched the girl's shoulder in order to turn her around.

A horrific face gazed back at her.

The first thing Terri noticed were her blood-red lips—so colored because they were, in fact, covered with blood.

Then she noticed the milky white eyes.

Both contrasted eerily with the pale skin.

The girl was dead.

Terri backed up. "Oh, my God!"

It wasn't the sight of the girl that truly frightened her, though.

It was the doll.

Or, rather, not a doll, but another little kid, off whom the girl had just fed.

Terri Morales had a strong stomach, and had managed to get through this day without throwing up.

Now, though, at the sight of one child feeding off another, her stomach lurched.

She bumped into something. At first she thought it was one of the desks, but when she turned around, she saw that it was a boy.

Another walking corpse.

Looking around the classroom, she saw that there were dozens of them.

All little kids.

All dead.

All with blood on their lips.

All moving in on her.

They literally had her cornered. There was no way out of the room now. From all sides came the army of dead children.

The boy grabbed her right arm and bit it.

Terri screamed.

Another one grabbed her leg.

A third bit her right on the hip.

The pain was overwhelming, as hundreds of small teeth ripped into her flesh.

She could have used her gun, but how could she shoot little kids?

Instead, she screamed louder, even as the gun fell to the floor.

Her rent legs could no longer support her weight, and she fell to the floor, the kiddie corpses swarming all over her now-prone form.

The last thing she saw was her camera, which was lying on one of the desks at an odd angle, still recording.

Her last thought was that the only way she'd get that Emmy now was posthumously.

✝WE∩✝Y-SIX

Angela Ashford had seen her first dead body today.

In fact, she'd seen her first two this morning. It was after the car crash.

The big truck had crashed into the SUV that the two men who took her out of class were driving.

The two men had died in the crash.

Angela knew this even though she'd never seen a dead body, because she tried to wake them both up, but they weren't breathing and didn't move and were covered with blood.

Her third dead body was the driver of the truck, who was all smelly. Angela knew from her science class that bodies got smelly after they'd been dead for a while. He also had a big hole in his chest.

The only reason Angela was still alive was because

she had put on her seat belt. Her chest kinda hurt from when the seat belt pulled against her in the crash, but at least she didn't go flying through the windshield like one man did, or get crushed under the roof like the other one.

It was tough to get out of the car, but she managed it. She still clutched her Spider-Man lunchbox. That was, she knew, the most important thing of all.

She went back to school. Mr. Strunk would know what to do about the car crash. And if he didn't, Principal Armin would.

But then the truck driver followed her back to the school.

Which didn't make sense, because the truck driver was dead.

True, Angela hadn't seen any dead bodies before today, but she did watch television and she saw movies and she had paid attention in science class.

If you weren't breathing and had a hole in your chest, you were dead.

Which meant he'd been turned into a monster.

The truck driver—who was a grown-up, so he had longer legs—made it back to the school faster than Angela did.

The vice-principal, Ms. Rosenthal, was talking with her secretary, Ms. Garcia, in the hallway when the truck driver walked in. Angela was just a little bit behind him.

"Excuse me, sir, you can't be in he—"

Ms. Rosenthal cut herself off when she saw the big hole in the truck driver's chest.

Angela screamed when the truck driver bit Ms. Rosenthal on the neck.

Ms. Garcia ran away. Principal Armin came out of his office.

"What's going on here?" Then he saw the truck driver. "Oh, my God."

When the truck driver walked over to Principal Armin, he said a very bad word.

Then the truck driver bit him, too.

Ms. Rosenthal got up a second later. She looked all funny. The truck driver had turned her into a monster, too.

Angela walked up to her and asked her if she was okay. But the vice-principal didn't say anything, didn't even pay any attention to Angela.

Instead, she and the truck driver started walking down the hall together.

Pretty soon, Principal Armin did the same thing.

For the next several hours, it got worse.

Principal Armin went into Mr. Strunk's class and bit him. All the kids panicked, but the truck driver and Ms. Rosenthal and one of the janitors and the two men in the gray suits, all of whom were monsters now, all got in their way and started biting them.

In homeroom, Angela Ashford had told Bobby Bernstein that she hoped he'd die.

By midmorning, she got to watch it happen.

The other kids tried hiding in the basement, but soon the monsters found them and turned them into more monsters. Soon, the monsters far outnumbered the kids.

But they all left Angela alone.

She didn't understand it. What was so special about her? Was it because of what Daddy had done to her to make her not be crippled anymore?

Sometime during the day, a truck crashed into the school. The writing on the side said it belonged to the Raccoon City Police Department's Canine Unit. The truck was carrying a bunch of dogs.

They were monsters now, too.

By nightfall, monster kids, monster teachers, monster janitors, and monster dogs were wandering all over the school. The dogs were mostly prowling around the cafeteria, with the other monsters roaming around the rest of the school.

They still left Angela alone.

After a while she realized why: whatever it was that Daddy had used to cure her also was responsible for what had happened here today. She wasn't sure how she knew this, but she was more sure of it than she was of anything.

Besides, it explained why the monsters wouldn't touch her.

Because she was a monster, too.

The monsters wouldn't leave the other five people alone, the ones who came later. There were the two men in black, and then the two women and the funny-dressed man. Angela saw them from where she was hiding on the roof, clutching her lunchbox.

After a minute, she decided to go downstairs and see if they could help her—or if she could help them, and keep them from becoming monsters.

Angela saw as they took one of the women away. She was too late to save her.

Another woman, the one wearing the blue top, came in after the monsters took the first woman away. This woman carried a gun.

"You can't help her. Not now."

The woman turned around, holding up the gun.

"I've seen what they do."

Lowering the gun, the woman asked, "Are you Angela?"

Angela nodded. "We should hurry, before they come back."

The woman saw something on the floor and picked it up. It looked like some kind of video camera. Angela supposed it belonged to the other woman.

She'd be a monster soon.

"My name's Jill. Your father sent me to find you."

Relief spread over Angela. She *knew* Daddy would find a way to save her!

Jill led her out into the corridor.

"Angela Ashford—that's a pretty grown-up name for a little girl."

"I'm nine years old, I'm not a little girl."

"I see."

"Besides," Angela muttered, "everyone calls me Angie."

"Angie. I like that."

Normally, Angela hated it when grown-ups called her that. But when Jill said it, she kinda liked it.

They turned toward the cafeteria.

Angela stopped.

"We can't go through there."

"It's okay, honey, this is the quickest route."

"No! Those things are in there!"

Jill took Angela's hand. It felt warm and comforting.

"It's okay. They're slow—we can run around them."

Sure enough, as they entered the cafeteria, there were a few of the monsters roaming around.

They looked up as she and Jill entered.

But that wasn't what Angela was worried about. "No, not them." She pointed at one of the dog monsters. "Them."

The dog was hunched over yet another dead body. It was Ms. Modzelewski.

Angela would have cried for her favorite homeroom teacher, but she'd run out of tears hours ago.

With a growl, the dog monster charged Jill.

Jill raised her gun and shot the monster, but it still crashed into her. Jill fell down, and her gun went skidding across the floor and into the kitchen area.

Even though the dog monster had been shot, it was still moving.

Angela ran for cover. She couldn't watch. She'd seen enough people die, she didn't want to make a new friend and watch *her* die, too.

Then she heard a sound like a thousand drumbeats. After a minute, she realized it was machine-gun fire, like in the movies.

A deep voice with a funny accent said, "Thought you might need a hand."

Then Jill said, "You work for Umbrella."

That was Daddy's company!

"Used to—till they left us for dead in this place. Now I consider myself freelance. Nicholai Sokolov at your service."

This must have been one of the two men in black.

But then Angela heard a lot of other noises— screams, bumps, growls. She risked looking up.

Mr. Sokolov was being torn to pieces by a bunch of dog monsters.

Jill was okay, though. Angela ran up and grabbed her leg. As long as the dog monsters were focused on Mr. Sokolov, they might be able to escape.

"Come on! This way!"

Angela led them into the kitchen. There were more places to hide in there, and most of the dog monsters were out in the cafeteria.

Besides, Jill's gun was there.

There were only two dog monsters in the kitchen, both on the far side from the stove Jill had chosen for them to hide behind.

Jill put a finger to her lips. Angela nodded. She knew to be quiet.

With any luck, they'd get out and she'd see Daddy soon.

They got very close to Jill's gun. So far, the dog monsters hadn't seen them. But if she reached for the gun, she'd be out in the open. Jill hesitated.

Angela was scared.

Then Ms. Gorfinkle, the lunch lady, grabbed Jill. Angela hadn't seen her coming. Ms. Gorfinkle was a monster now, too, of course.

Every person who'd been attacked by a monster became a monster. But Jill didn't—instead, she got Ms. Gorfinkle in a headlock and then did something that made an awful snapping noise.

Ms. Gorfinkle fell to the floor.

"Okay?" Jill whispered to Angela.

Angela gave Jill an "okay" sign with her fingers. She liked her new friend a lot.

They were hunkered down by one of the stoves. Unfortunately, one of the dog monsters was now standing over Jill's gun.

Jill looked up at the stoves.

Then she smiled.

She turned on each of the burners. Angela could hear the whooshing sound of the gas—and she could smell it, too.

The dog monster started sniffing the air. Angela knew from science class that dogs had better senses of smell than humans, and she figured monster ones did, too. If she could smell the gas, so could the dog monsters.

Jill reached into her pocket and pulled out a book of matches.

Then she grabbed Angela's arm and they ran for the cafeteria.

As they ran, Jill lit one of the matches without removing it from the book, then tossed it behind her.

Angela glanced back to watch as she ran away.

Daddy had always told her that it was dangerous to light a match near a stove burner because the gas would catch fire. But now, Jill *wanted* the gas to catch fire to stop the dog monsters.

The book of matches was ablaze. It tumbled through the air.

The dog monsters were heading for them.

The matches went out.

Before they hit the gas.

The dog monsters kept coming.

Angela heard a slight hissing sound. She looked up to see a cigarette flying through the air, which was weird, since nobody was allowed to smoke in the building.

A blond woman was standing in the doorway. Angela didn't think she had ever seen her before, but she looked kinda familiar anyhow. The woman grabbed Angela and protected her in the folds of the coat she was wearing.

Angela felt the heat of the explosion through the woman's coat, heard the sound of it slam into her ears.

After a moment, the woman unfurled her coat.

"Thank you," Angela said to her savior.

Jill was on the floor, which was weird, since the blond woman had managed to remain standing.

"Nice of you to show up, Alice," Jill said. "You're making a habit of showing up in the nick of time to save my ass."

But the woman—Alice—wasn't listening to Jill. She was staring at Angela.

Angela stared back.

Somehow—with the same clarity with which Angela knew why the monsters were ignoring her—Angela knew that Alice was like her.

Had Daddy helped her, too?

"You two know each other?" Jill asked.

"She's infected," Alice said. "On a massive level."

Jill frowned. "How can you know that?"

Angela answered the question. "Because she is, too. Don't worry, I know how strange it must feel."

Whirling on Alice, Jill started yelling, "Wait a second! You're infected? And when were you going to tell me that?"

Alice kept ignoring Jill, which Angela didn't think was very nice. Instead, she stared at Angela's lunchbox.

"Let me see." Alice held out her hand.

"No!" Daddy had told her never to *ever* let that lunchbox out of her sight.

But Alice took it anyhow, yanking it away from Angela.

She popped open the box, to reveal what Angela kept with her at all times because Daddy had told her to.

Some kind of gray foam took up most of the inside, protecting four fancy needles. Daddy called them syringes—he also called them really really important.

"This is the antivirus," Alice said. "The cure to the T-virus."

"There's a *cure?*" Jill asked.

Alice nodded, then looked at Angela. "Isn't that right?"

Angela didn't say anything.

"How did you get this?"

At first, Angela didn't say anything. Then Alice closed the lunchbox and handed it back to her. As she took it, she decided to tell them the whole story. Jill said Daddy had sent her, after all, and they had both saved her life.

"My daddy—my daddy made it for me. He's sick, and someday I'll get sick, too. He just wanted to stop that. When I was little, I had to walk on crutches. They said I'd never get better, just worse. Then I'd be in a wheelchair, just like Daddy. But he found a way to make me stronger."

Jill cocked her head. "The T-virus."

Angela nodded. "But they took his invention away from him. The men at Umbrella. I've heard him crying, too, at night, when he thinks no one is listening. But I've heard him. He's not a bad man, you see. He didn't mean for any of this to happen. Honest."

Tears started to well up in Angela's eyes. She'd thought she was out of tears, but knowing she was finally going to see her daddy . . .

"Honest."

She collapsed into Alice's arms.

"I believe you," Alice said. "It's okay. It's going to be okay."

Then Angela heard the sound of a door slamming open. Alice was suddenly holding a shotgun and pointing it at the door.

But there was also a red light shining on Alice's chest.

Angela looked at the front of the room to see a man holding a big gun with a red light on it.

The man with the gun was wearing the same all-black uniform as Mr. Sokolov. "Don't point that at me unless you intend to use it."

He spoke, so he wasn't a monster.

"He's cool!" said another voice. The man who dressed funny and who'd come in with Jill and the other woman who was dead now walked up behind the man with the gun. "He be cool. He made a deal with Dr. Doom, same as you."

Jill looked at the man in black. Angela could now see a name tag on his chest that said OLIVERA. "How many of you guys are there?"

"What do you mean?" Mr. Olivera asked.

Then Mr. Olivera saw the body of Mr. Sokolov and his head sank.

"Nicholai . . ." he whispered.

Angela was tired of looking at dead bodies.

She wanted her daddy.

"When were you bitten?" Alice asked.

Now Angela looked at Mr. Olivera more closely. He looked all pale and sick.

"Two hours ago."

Angela held up the Spider-Man lunchbox.

Alice smiled. "It's your lucky day."

"Nobody's having a lucky day in this town today, Alice," Mr. Olivera said. "Don't know if you remember me—Carlos Olivera." He looked down at Angela. "I'm guessing this is the package we were both sent to pick up?"

"Looks like. Dr. Ashford obviously likes to hedge his bets."

"He works for Umbrella, of *course* he's hedging his bets."

Jill said, "Don't you two work for Umbrella?"

Both Alice and Mr. Olivera said, *"Used* to," at the same time. Angela felt a funny urge to giggle.

"Whatever. Let's get the hell out of here. I've got a truck parked outside, we can give him his shot there."

"I heard *that,*" the funny-dressed man said. "We just gots to find the pretty TV lady."

"The 'pretty TV lady' is dead," Jill said.

"What? *Bull*shit! She can't be dead, she's a celebrity!"

"Afraid so." Jill pulled the video camera out of her pocket. "All we've got is her legacy."

"Damn. There goes *my* chance at stardom."

†WEП†Y-SEVEП

Charles Ashford wondered when it was, exactly, that he'd lost his soul.

Was it a gradual process, he wondered, or had the Umbrella Corporation just eaten away at it like vultures picking over a corpse until there was nothing left but dry bones?

He had had the noblest of intentions, of course. There were so many things to learn, so many break-throughs to accomplish—but in order to do that, one needed resources.

Umbrella had deeper pockets than anyone else in the world. Only they could fund his research; only they could take that research to the next level; only they could apply it to real-world solutions beyond the theo-retical gosh-wow-wouldn't-it-be-great-if-we-could-do-this stage of lab work that had been Ashford's frustrating status quo until he was hired by Umbrella.

Umbrella also didn't care about his degenerative nerve condition. Ashford had never understood why, in a world where Stephen Hawking was the world's most famous living scientist, a man in a wheelchair would have so much trouble getting funding for his scientific work. Yet on dozens of occasions he'd had sure-thing grants and projects kicked out from under him right after the parties in question learned of his disability.

It was maddening.

More maddening was that he had passed on the condition to his daughter.

The T-virus was going to be his greatest creation. Yes, it would be used for a wrinkle cream, as much so it could be a test case as anything, a practical application to a wide range of people with minimal consequences if it failed.

But it was also the key to a cure for so many diseases.

Especially the one suffered by both Ashford and his daughter.

Angie would get to lead a normal life.

Or, at least, that was what he had thought.

Ashford knew something was wrong when they moved the T-virus research down to the Hive—and cut him out of it. Instead, they put those two sex-crazed young people, Mariano Rodriguez and Anna Bolt, in charge. Decent scientists, both of them, with promising futures, but they were young and impulsive.

And, Ashford soon realized, much easier to manipulate.

Now it had all gone to hell.

In fact, it had gone to the ninth circle of hell, and there wasn't a damn thing Charles Ashford could do about it.

The only thing he could do was save his daughter. That had become his sole goal. He knew he couldn't do anything to stop Cain and his gun-toting goons from making a bad situation worse in Raccoon City. Ashford was well enough protected by his connections to Umbrella's board of directors—another recipient of the tattered remains of his soul—to keep Cain more or less off his back, but that protection certainly didn't allow him to take Cain on.

A lifetime of being forced to sit meant that Ashford spent a great deal of time in front of a computer. Though he wouldn't call himself a class-A hacker by any means, he knew his way around the machines well enough that, given his high-level access to Umbrella's mainframe, he could navigate around the system with impunity. That often involved tying his laptop in to the Umbrella-built cameras located all over the city, ostensibly for the police department's use. Ashford knew that Umbrella used them for whatever suited its purposes at any given time.

Right now, Ashford was using them to rescue his daughter.

Mobile phone service was being jammed by Cain, but he couldn't affect the land lines belonging to Verizon. Ashford had been able to tie his own satellite phone—a perk of his position—into the pay-phone network throughout the city.

He knew that, even in so obscene a postapocalyptic scenario as that playing out in Raccoon City, there would be survivors—those hardy enough to endure under even the worst of circumstances. He had found several in Alice Abernathy and Carlos Olivera, both members of Umbrella's Security Division, as well as Officer Jill Valentine of the police department's S.T.A.R.S. unit. In truth, Valentine was the only one he trusted, but he knew they were all motivated by a desire to survive. Umbrella had abandoned all of them to their deaths. Ashford was throwing them a lifeline.

They weren't likely to give that up.

To his irritation, there were no cameras in the school proper that he could tap, so he was forced to maintain a vigil on the traffic camera at the corner of Hudson and Robertson.

Eventually, after an interminable wait, he saw Officer Valentine, Abernathy, and Olivera emerge, plus that black fellow who was tagging along—

—and Angie! They'd done it!

"Thank God," Ashford muttered to himself.

He noticed that neither the television reporter nor Sokolov came out. That was a tragedy, true—though, from what Ashford had seen on the morning news, the loss of Terri Morales was not one that would be widely mourned by any rational television viewer—but given the events of this day, they would have died 'ere long, as the Bard would say. All Ashford cared about was getting his daughter back.

After tapping several keys that linked his phone to the pay phone near the playground behind the school, Ashford dialed it.

He watched on the monitor as Abernathy and the others reacted to it.

As soon as Abernathy picked up the phone, Ashford said, "Let me speak to my daughter."

"First you tell us how we're getting out."

Angrily, Ashford said, "Don't try to make deals with me."

Then Abernathy hung up the phone.

Ashford blinked.

Who the hell did that woman think she was? He was offering her a way out—a way to *survive,* even as the rest of the city died around her! How *dare* she treat him like some kind of common criminal!

He blinked again.

Wasn't he a common criminal? After all, accessory to murder was a criminal act, and by creating the T-virus, he was one. The law probably would never prosecute him as such—Umbrella paid good money to a lot of lawyers to prevent its higher-ups from ever having to face anything as irrelevant as a consequence—but that didn't change the facts.

Ashford redialed the number.

Abernathy let it ring five times before picking up.

"We understand each other?"

"There's a helicopter already being prepped. It takes

off in—" Ashford checked the time stamp in the corner of his monitor "—forty-seven minutes. It'll be the last transport to leave Raccoon City."

"I take it this helicopter isn't laid on especially for us?"

Ashford smiled. "No. It has another purpose, but it will be lightly guarded."

"Where's the evac site?"

Now Ashford had to draw the line. "First I talk to Angie."

To Ashford's relief, this time Abernathy capitulated. She handed the phone to Angie.

"Daddy!"

At the sound of his little girl, alive and well, even sounding vaguely chipper, which was nothing short of miraculous, Charles Ashford felt true joy for the first time in years.

Probably for the first time since Angie's mother died.

"I'm here," he said in a quiet voice.

"When can I see you?"

Not soon enough, Ashford thought, but he wanted to be encouraging for his little girl. "It's okay, baby. These people are going to bring you to me. I'll see you real soon."

"I hope so, Daddy. I want you to meet my new friends."

Ashford shuddered. These were not the kind of people he wanted his daughter befriending.

On the other hand, they were still alive in a city full

of the walking dead. How could she not bond with the first living beings she'd seen all day? Especially the ones who were bringing her back to her father?

"Angie, could you please put Ms. Abernathy back on the phone?"

"Okay, Daddy. I love you."

"I love you, too, sweetheart."

Abernathy came back on the line. "Well?"

"The helicopter will be at City Hall. I advise you to make haste—you only have forty-three minutes." He smiled. "You can take heart, though—the traffic should be light."

"We'll see you soon, Doctor," was all Abernathy said in reply.

Then she hung up.

With a goofy grin on his face—a gesture he wouldn't have believed himself capable of an hour ago—he watched as the five of them walked to the pickup truck that Officer Valentine had liberated earlier.

A minute later, they were on the road, heading up Hudson in the general direction of City Hall. Ashford changed his view from traffic camera to traffic camera as they proceeded.

Then the laptop screen flickered and went dark.

"What the hell—?"

He tapped several keys in rapid succession, but nothing. The connection had gone dead.

But it was a T3 line. Normally, it would be wireless, but the same method being used to jam mobile phones would have scrambled a wireless signal, so all the network connections in the base camp were hardwired.

"Computers," said a familiar, German-accented voice behind him. "So unreliable. Just like people."

Cain.

Ashford turned his wheelchair around to find Timothy Cain, given the appallingly inappropriate nickname of "Able," holding a knife and the cut T3 cable.

"You really thought I didn't know about your little one-man insurrection?"

"It's not an insurrection," Ashford said through gritted teeth. "I just want my daughter back."

"Your daughter is a casualty. She became one the minute we closed the doors at the bridge. Now, it's regrettable that your little girl is going to die, Doctor, it truly is. But what's even more regrettable is that, by doing what you're doing, you've signed your own death warrant as well."

Ashford found himself chuckling involuntarily at that.

"Something amuses you, Doctor?"

"Not especially, Cain, it's just that—until I met you, I didn't think real people talked like that."

Cain walked to the rear of Ashford's chair and started wheeling him out of the tent. "What you don't know about real people, Doctor, is considerable. But you're about to get a very nasty lesson."

✝WEП✝Y-EİGH✝

Once the truck got going, Alice, sitting in the narrow backseat with Carlos and Angie, asked the girl for her lunchbox.

"I need to inject Carlos with the antivirus."

Angie nodded and handed it over.

"Thanks," Alice said with a warm smile.

She didn't think very highly of the girl's father. After all, he was the one who'd first developed the T-virus. From what she knew of the project, it had been taken out of his purview in fairly short order, and the more reprehensible applications—the ones that had made the T-virus attractive enough for Spence Parks to steal—hadn't come into play until after that, but that didn't change the fact that he'd developed it.

Still and all, she was glad that she'd at least be able to reunite him with his little girl.

They should all be so lucky.

Carlos rolled up his sleeve, revealing a combat knife that he presumably kept there as emergency backup. "What is this stuff?"

Alice answered while she swabbed his arm and prepped the syringe. "The T-virus promotes cellular growth. It can reanimate dead cells, causing the dead to walk. Or in a living human, it can cause uncontrollable mutation. Or in a little girl with withered legs," she added with a wink at Angie, "it can help her walk again. *If* the virus is kept in check."

Frowning as Alice stuck the needle into his arm, Carlos said, "That little girl is infected?"

Alice nodded. "It's why the undead in the school didn't touch her. She's infected with the T-virus, just like them." She indicated the syringe. "But this keeps the virus under control. The cellular growth is just enough to keep her on her feet, but not quite enough to cause further mutation."

Valentine was up front driving. Next to her, that L.J. Wayne character Valentine had acquired was riding shotgun. Alice hadn't had time to get his story, but he came across as the typical know-nothing punk who somehow survived on the streets of every major city through a combination of attitude and dumb luck.

It was Valentine who asked, "And they infected you with this T-virus as well?"

"Yes."

Carlos looked at her in shock.

She continued, "They made me one of their little monsters."

"So if you're infected," Valentine said, "why did those creatures attack you in the cemetery?"

"They didn't." Alice smiled wryly. "They attacked *you*. I just got in their way. I'd already learned that they had no interest in me. When I was wandering the streets, before I found you in the church, I encountered a whole bunch of them—but they left me completely alone. Even the biker I took the motorcycle from didn't attack."

Carlos had by now rolled down his sleeve and replaced the knife, and was starting to look almost lifelike. "That's quite a story."

Angie asked, "But if you're sick, too, why don't you have to take the medicine?"

Alice shook her head. "I don't know."

"Here."

Looking up at Valentine's single word, Alice saw that the cop was handing back a small metal object.

Taking it, Alice realized it was Terri Morales's little video camera. She'd had the thing on constantly as they'd moved through the city. It was probably the best record in existence of the day's events.

Checking the playback, Alice saw that the last thing it had recorded was Terri's own death.

Shaking her head, Alice looked up to see Valentine giving her a look in the rearview mirror.

"I'll see that it gets put to good use."

Then Alice understood.

Valentine was a cop, and cops thought in terms of evidence that could be presented in a court of law. Evidence usually took two forms: physical evidence and eyewitness testimony.

As good as physical evidence was, it wasn't always enough, particularly if there could be doubt as to its authenticity.

Valentine wanted the testimony. She wanted the confession. And Alice was the only one who could provide it.

Pointing the recorder at her own face, she hit the RECORD button and started talking.

"My name is Alice Abernathy. I worked for the Umbrella Corporation." She hesitated, then added, "The largest and most powerful commercial entity in the world." Let everyone know that she was well aware of who, precisely, it was she was fucking with, and didn't care.

This was too big.

"I was head of security at the high-tech Umbrella facility named the Hive—a giant underground laboratory that was developing, among other things, experimental viral weaponry."

Alice hesitated. Did she want to get into Spence's malfeasance here?

No, there was little point. Spence was dead, and the identity of his potential buyer or buyers had died with him. There was nothing to be gained by blaming him when he'd already paid the ultimate price—and that would distract from the important part.

"But there was an accident. The virus escaped and everyone in the laboratory—five hundred people, all employees of the Umbrella Corporation—died."

She hesitated again. Regardless of the number of times she'd witnessed it since she first saw the reanimated corpses shuffling toward her in the Hive's "dining hall," she still had trouble believing the truth of their situation.

"But they didn't *stay* dead. The T-virus reanimated their bodies—brought the dead back to life, and left them with a terrible hunger for the flesh of the living."

God, that sounded like the copy on the DVD case of a shitty 1950s B-movie.

Yet, it was the truth. And the truth was what she needed to tell, and she could not afford to soft-pedal it.

"I glimpsed hell, saw things I cannot describe."

Unbidden, images from her sojourn through the Hive came back to her, from the lasers cutting One, Drew, Warner, and Danilova to pieces to the endless swarms of undead creatures chasing them through the Hive's halls and ductwork to the licker grabbing poor Kaplan and ripping him to shreds to Matt being forced to shoot Rain in the head—

—to the streets of Raccoon City being turned into one huge graveyard.

"But I survived. Myself and one other—a man named Matt Addison. When we emerged from the lab, we were seized by Umbrella scientists. Matt and I were separated."

Alice took a deep breath.

"We thought that it was over. We thought that we had survived the horror. But we were wrong. The nightmare had only just begun."

Another hesitation, and this time she looked up to see the expressions on the faces of Carlos and Angie.

Until now, they hadn't known the true extent of what had gone on in the Hive. Alice wondered if it would have been better if they had not found out—especially poor Angie, who had been through more than any nine-year-old girl should.

But they needed that confession.

"Recorded here is footage taken by Terri Morales of Raccoon 7 before she, too, was killed. The Umbrella Corporation may try to cover this up. All I can say is, don't listen to them. They are responsible for this. Millions of people have already died because of their carelessness. They have to be stopped."

Alice hit the STOP button.

From the front of the truck, Wayne said, "A-fuckin'-men to *that*."

Carlos snorted. "Yeah, what he said."

Again, silence descended upon the truck.

Then Angie leaned over and gave Alice a hug.

Closing her eyes and letting out a breath she hadn't even realized she was holding, Alice gratefully returned the hug.

"We're almost at City Hall," Valentine said. "Let's get ready to roll."

Valentine parked the truck a block away from City Hall, which was a smoking ruin.

Carlos had a pair of binoculars. He climbed to the roof of the truck and peered through them.

"There it is. A C89 in the square, right next to the fountain. It's surrounded by three guards, and they're surrounded by a bunch of glass sheets that are probably supposed to keep the riffraff out. Hell, that's gotta be that PlastiGlas stuff Umbrella developed—bulletproof, and probably zombieproof, too." He lowered the binoculars. "Lightly guarded. Right."

Wayne held up his Uzi. "Four of us, three of them."

"Actually," Carlos said, "four of them. I don't see anyone, but I'm sure there's a sniper on the roof. There always is."

"What-the-fuck-ever, dog—let's kick some *ass*."

"Down, boy," Valentine said to Wayne, then looked up at Carlos. "How are they armed?"

"MP5Ks."

"Probably with a full load of ammo. We've got a bunch of popguns by comparison, and we're all starting to run low. We'll have our heads handed to us."

"I'll take care of them," Alice said.

"Oh, you will, will you?"

Valentine sounded skeptical. Even after the church and the school, she didn't truly appreciate how good Alice was.

"Yes, I will. There won't be a shot fired."

In fact, Alice wasn't entirely sure she herself appreciated how good she was.

Whatever it was Umbrella had done unto her,

though, she was about to do it right back unto their miserable faces.

Minutes later, Alice had worked her way onto what remained of the City Hall roof. As Carlos had predicted, there was a sniper posted there, complete with a full set of rappelling gear, just in case he needed to make a hasty exit to the street. All standard.

And about to become exceedingly useful.

The first thing she did was take out the sniper. This proved wise, as the sniper was setting up a head shot on Carlos, who was approaching the square with Valentine. Wayne had been left behind to guard Angie until they gave the signal. Wayne had objected to this part of the plan at great length, right up until Valentine described, in graphic detail, what she would do to his spleen if he didn't shut up and do what they said.

Alice was really starting to like Jill Valentine.

Once the sniper was disposed of, Alice unspooled the cable and dropped it down into the square, between the C89 and the three guards.

The guards didn't notice—their attention was, understandably, focused outward. That was where the true danger lay, after all—from the legions of undead that could come shuffling toward them, and might not be stopped by the PlastiGlas barrier.

Alice attached a hook to the cable, then attached the hook to her coat. Leaving her weapons holstered, she slid down the cable, stopping herself just short of the square.

The guards turned around at the zipperlike sound of the steel hook sliding along the metallic cable, but before they had a chance to react, Alice went at them.

First, she snapped a guard's neck.

Then she drove the heel of her left hand into the nose of the second one, breaking it and sending shards of cartilage and bone into his brain, killing him instantly.

Finally, she smashed the third one's throat with her right hand.

The third one died before the first one even had a chance to hit the ground.

By the time the third one hit the ground, Carlos and Valentine had arrived.

After squeezing between two of the PlastiGlas sheets, Carlos suddenly whipped out his combat knife and threw it past Alice.

Whirling around, Alice saw that the second guard wasn't as dead as he was supposed to be. He hadn't been made undead—his eyes were clear, and he said, "Fuck!" when Carlos's knife hit his chest—but apparently the shards of skull hadn't penetrated his brain as deeply as she'd thought.

"Missed one," Carlos said with a smile.

Shrugging, Alice said, "Had to leave something for you to do."

Valentine rolled her eyes. "You two can pull your pants down and compare sizes later." Sticking her pinky fingers into her mouth, she whistled.

Alice winced. The piercing noise of the whistle sliced through her now-ultra-sensitive ears.

Seconds later, Wayne and Angie came running.

"*Nice* work," Wayne said.

"Let's go," Alice said quickly. She didn't want Angie to linger around dead bodies any more than she had to.

Any more than she already had.

They entered the helicopter's cargo area, and Alice found herself immediately overwhelmed by a feeling of déjà vu.

Sitting in the center of the cargo area were two large diagnostic beds.

One was a dead ringer for the one in which she'd woken up at Raccoon City Hospital.

The other looked like the first one, only with a pituitary problem. Instinctively, Alice knew who it was intended for:

Nemesis.

Ashford had never told her what this transport was for. Now she knew: it was to get her and Nemesis out of the city before it was nuked.

"What is all this?" Valentine asked.

"We have to hurry," was all Alice would say in reply.

If Umbrella wanted to get them out of town, it meant that Nemesis could be here any minute. She'd barely escaped with her life the last time she faced him; she had no confidence in being so lucky this time.

"It's okay," Carlos said, looking at the sky. Sunrise was still about twenty minutes away. "We still have time, we're going to make it."

Alice looked out the open cargo door. Without even needing to think about it, she knew where to look.

She pointed to a distant roof.

"No, we *have* to hurry."

The others followed her gaze to see what she saw.

A giant figure standing on a rooftop, holding a rail gun.

Nemesis.

Wayne's eyes nearly popped out of his head. "We be stealin' *his* ride? Sheeeee-it!"

"I'll get us in the air." Alice unholstered her Colt .45 and moved to the cockpit.

Opening the sliding door, she saw a man in the same all-black Umbrella commando outfit that Carlos—and One, Rain, Kaplan, and the others—wore.

"Take off."

The pilot didn't move.

Alice put the Colt's muzzle to his head.

"Now."

The pilot smiled, but still didn't move.

"I said, now!"

"What's the hurry?"

Alice whirled around, holding up the Colt.

It was Cain.

He had a weapon of his own, a Glock pressed right up against Angie Ashford's head.

"Come with me, please."

Alice noted that Cain didn't ask her to drop her weapons. Not that it mattered—she wasn't going to do anything as long as Angie's life was in danger.

She had only been gone a few seconds, but in that time an entire team of Cain's security people had moved in and gotten the drop on Valentine, Carlos, and Wayne.

They were on their knees in the City Hall square, along with a middle-aged man Alice didn't recognize.

Angie, however, did.

"Daddy!"

Cain removed the weapon from Angie's head, and she ran to her father. Both teary-eyed, they hugged each other, Ashford still on his knees.

"Angie."

"I knew you wouldn't leave me," Angie said between sobs.

"Never, baby, never."

"Did they hurt you?"

"No." Ashford was lying through his teeth, Alice could tell that much just by looking at him. "No, I'm okay, baby."

Alice looked over to see a Darkwing stealth chopper that had arrived without her noticing. The same kind that One had used to arrive at the mansion shortly after Alice woke up amnesiac during the Hive mess—she hadn't heard that, either.

Cain's people were handcuffing Valentine, Carlos, and Wayne.

As the latter was cuffed, he muttered, "Shit, man, déjà-motherfuckass-vu."

The one cuffing Valentine asked, "What shall we do with them, sir?"

Alice heard the sound of heavy footfalls growing closer.

Nemesis was coming.

"Not a goddamn thing," Cain said. "They'll be dead

soon enough. Just enough time for us to finish our little experiment."

As Cain spoke, Nemesis entered the square, leaping over the PlastiGlas that held back an increasing number of undead.

"The viral outbreak, while regrettable, did provide an excellent test scenario for the Nemesis Program."

Alice shot Cain a look. She'd known him long enough to be aware just how reprehensible a bastard he was, but even by his standards, calling the day's events "regrettable" was beyond the pale.

Cain, meanwhile, indicated Nemesis with an almost theatrical gesture. "The perfect soldier."

They stood face to face now, Alice and Nemesis. Neither one of them moving. For the second time, Alice felt more than saw Nemesis, their heartbeats matching in perfect unison.

"You two showed such promise." Cain kept droning—he always had liked the sound of his own voice. "But we had to see you in action. And most impressive you've been." He looked at each of them in turn. "That's right. Can you feel it?"

Hesitantly, Alice said, "I feel . . ." She trailed off, unable to think of a way to quantify it.

Cain finished the sentence for her: "Kinship. You're like brother and sister. Heightened speed, strength, agility. The same killer instincts." He smiled. "Just in a slightly more attractive package. But under the skin, you're almost identical. Parallel strands of research. And now we discover which is superior."

Throughout, Nemesis had stood unmoving, an eight-foot-tall statue. The only movement came from the occasional blinking of his blue eyes.

Blue eyes.

That seemed wrong somehow.

And yet very familiar.

Alice looked away, toward Valentine and the others.

She and Carlos locked eyes for a moment.

Almost imperceptibly, Carlos nodded.

Good. While the Umbrella troops had taken the handguns, they hadn't done a thorough search. He still literally had something up his sleeve: the knife, retrieved from the guard he'd killed earlier.

Cain, meanwhile, turned toward Nemesis. "Discard primary weaponry."

The sound of Nemesis dropping the rocket launcher and rail gun to the pavement echoed off the PlastiGlas.

"Now kill her."

It took less than a second. One moment, Nemesis was doing his statue impersonation.

The next, he was charging her.

But, as fast as he was, Alice was faster. She dodged the frontal assault with little difficulty.

He attacked again. She dodged again, but did not attack.

This kept up for several minutes. Alice just needed to stall until Carlos could free his knife and himself.

Cain, however, was starting to look pissed.

"Fight him!"

"No." Alice had no intention of hurting Nemesis if

she didn't have to. Whoever he was, he was as much a victim as she was.

Unholstering his Glock, Cain said, "Fight him, or they die."

Shit.

Alice should have expected Cain to pull that tactic.

But then, he didn't know how much she cared one way or the other. So she tried a bluff.

"What makes you think I care?"

Without any hesitation, Cain pulled the trigger.

Ashford fell to the ground, blood pooling around his head.

Angie screamed, "Daddy!"

Cain pointed the Glock at Valentine.

"He was a valuable asset to the corporation. I don't even *care* about these people."

Grinding her teeth, Alice nodded and moved to face Nemesis.

Lowering his weapon, Cain said, "Begin."

When Alice had first started taking martial arts courses as a teenager in Columbus, Ohio, her sensei had told her that the truly great fighters enter into a trance where they shut out everything but their own movements. "One does not think. One simply does." Such great fighters, however, were rare. Perhaps one in a million.

He'd told her this, he said, because he saw a greatness in her that might someday allow her to be one of those one-in-a-million fighters.

With the aid of Umbrella's tampering, Alice had become more than that.

Once before on this night she had come close to entering this trance: in the graveyard behind the church on Dilmore Place, when the undead came rising from their graves.

Now it happened again.

She moved.

Of the collateral damage to the square, she was wholly unaware, though she vaguely knew it had to be tremendous. Nemesis's strength was monumental, and every blow that missed her struck a statue or a car or pavement or a kiosk.

Of the onlookers, she was equally unaware, though they probably suspected that she was losing, as her moves had become more and more defensive.

Nemesis backed her up against a wall.

Cornered.

A massive fist went straight for her head.

At the last second, she ducked it, then ran up Nemesis's chest and delivered a spinning heel-kick to his face, sending him crashing backward to the ground.

Anyone else's neck would have snapped.

Nemesis, however, was not anyone else.

Dazed, he grabbed a ten-foot piece of metal. Focused as she was, Alice had no idea where the metal came from—support beam, statue, vehicle debris, whatever.

What mattered was that Nemesis wielded it now like a sword.

She backflipped over his first thrust, which missed her by inches.

The second thrust came straight for her head just as she landed on her feet.

Flinging up her hands, she brought them together over the flat of the blade, stopping it just short of her head.

Her strength kept him from delivering the killing blow.

But his strength kept her from pushing the makeshift sword back into his chest.

At first.

Alice had lost some of sensei's focus, but she still had her anger. Since waking up naked in the shower of the mansion that led to the Hive, she had seen far too many people die. Lisa Broward. Rain Melendez. Bart Kaplan. Terri Morales. Peyton Wells. Charles Ashford.

She took her anger at the injustice of a world that allowed good people like Lisa and Rain and Kaplan and Wells and the others to die, yet allowed Timothy fucking Cain to live, and focused it into her considerable strength.

And she pushed.

Nemesis stumbled backward, a ten-foot piece of metal impaling him in the chest.

Pressing her advantage, Alice started pounding her fallen foe, each blow in revenge for Kaplan and Rain and Wells and the hundreds of others she didn't know who'd died just because Umbrella *had* to have a supervirus and Spence *had* to have his big payday and—

—and then she and Nemesis locked eyes.

Alice knew why the blue eyes were so familiar.

Matt!

✝WEN✝Y-ΠIΠE

Matthew Addison had been trying for hours to gain dominance over Nemesis.

Umbrella's programming was good. They had subsumed Matt's personality as far as they could, but they couldn't eliminate it altogether.

But every attempt to regain control of his own body had failed.

When they'd arrived at City Hall and Matt saw Alice once again, his spirit fell. He knew that Nemesis's primary objective was to seek out Alice and destroy her. He had already tried once, and only Alice's ingenuity and smaller size kept it from getting any uglier.

This time, though, Matt was going to try something else.

Memories.

Nemesis knew only his programming, but Matt knew where that programming came from.

He tried to force the images from his own mind onto Nemesis.

The times he'd come across the Umbrella Corporation during his tenure with the U.S. Marshals Service.

His growing frustration at his inability to pin any of its illicit activities on it.

Aaron Vricella recruiting him for the secret organization dedicated to bringing Umbrella down.

The years of greater frustration as his and Aaron's group failed to make headway, even as Umbrella's power and influence grew.

His suggesting using his sister Lisa, who had her own grudge against Umbrella, to infiltrate the company to try to find the evidence they needed.

The destruction of the Hive on the very day Lisa was to deliver the evidence to Matt, thanks to the greed of an asshole named Spence Parks.

Matt's sojourn through the devastated remains of the Hive, first as the prisoner of Umbrella's hired goons, then as one of the few survivors of the fruits of Spence's greed: five hundred undead creatures.

The attack of the licker on the train, wounding him and starting the mutation process.

Collapsing in the mansion's vestibule and being strapped down by Umbrella doctors in Hazmat suits.

Being experimented upon by a man named Sam Isaacs, the head of the Nemesis Program, and his superior, a total bastard named Major Timothy Cain.

Having his DNA rewritten, an agonizing process made worse by not being able to scream.

His own thoughts subsumed to a series of programming instructions written by Isaacs and supervised by Cain, forcing him to think of them as his masters.

Knowing that the very corporation he had dedicated his life to destroying had turned him into its ultimate weapon.

And right next to him, throughout the process, was Alice, having the same experiments done on her.

But, while Isaacs was turning Matt into a Frankenstein's monster, Alice remained herself. She was physically unchanged, at least on the outside.

Eventually, Matt got through.

Nemesis weakened.

Just in time for Alice to stab him in the chest.

And then for Alice to finally recognize who it was she had been fighting all this time.

With the same look of agony that Matt had seen on her face when Rain asked Alice to kill her if she mutated, Alice now whispered, "I'm sorry, Matt."

"Finish him." That was the voice that Nemesis knew only as his master, but Matt knew as Cain.

"No." Alice got up and took a step toward the master.

Toward Cain. Not the master. You're Matt Addison, not Nemesis!

Several of the master's—of *Cain's*—thugs raised their weapons, but Cain waved them down.

"No, no, it's okay." He looked at Alice. "Don't you

understand how important you are to us? That creature is one thing, but you? You're something very, very special. Somehow you bonded with the T-virus on a cellular level. You adapted *it,* you changed *it.* You became something magnificent."

That, Matt realized, was why she was left unchanged even as he got transformed into what Cain had so bluntly called a creature.

"I became a freak," Alice said.

No, Matt wanted to cry out. *I'm the freak, not her.*

"No, far from it," Cain said, and for once in his life Matt agreed with him. "You're not mutation, you're evolution."

Mutation is *part of evolution, you ignorant jackass!* But Matt still couldn't control his own vocal cords.

"Think about it. It took five million years for us to step out of the trees. You took the next step in less than five days. With our help, just think what you can achieve. Now, who can understand that? Who can appreciate that? Us—no one else. Where else are you going to go?"

Anywhere that has a conscience! This is why I've tried so hard to destroy you, you arrogant bastards!

"And what about him?" Alice asked, indicating Nemesis.

Cain just shrugged. "Evolution has its dead ends. Now finish this. Take your place at my side."

My God, he's not just a corporate asshole, he's a fucking megalomaniac.

"I understand," Cain said, "he was your friend." He

unholstered his Glock and held it out to Alice. "Here, do it clean."

Alice looked down at the weapon, then over at Nemesis.

At Matt.

"It's what he wants," Cain said.

Like hell.

"To be put out of his misery."

No, asshole, I want you *put out of my misery! For Christ's sake, Alice, don't do it!*

Alice raised the Glock. "Yes."

Then she turned and pointed the weapon at Cain and pulled the trigger.

Yes!

But all that came from the Glock was a dry click.

Empty.

No!

Cain smiled, and held up the Glock's ammo clip.

"All that strength, but no will to use it. What a waste. You're such a disappointment to me."

"You've no idea how happy that makes me." Matt could hear the contempt dripping from Alice's voice.

"Very well." Cain sighed and turned toward the pilot of the helicopter. "Prepare for takeoff."

Matt wanted more than anything else to get up and wipe that smirk off Cain's face.

To his surprise, his legs and body responded to that thought by clambering to his feet.

Hot shit.

Then he pulled the metal rod out of his chest.

Cain was still droning on. "You may be the superior warrior," he was saying to Alice, "but he is the superior soldier. He at least knows how to follow commands."

We'll just see about that, asshole.

Looking right at him, Cain said, "Kill her."

Matt didn't move.

"I said, kill her!"

Matt took a step toward Alice, which seemed to please Cain.

Then he went past her to where Nemesis had dropped the rail gun.

"What are you doing?"

What I've been wanting to do since you strapped me down in the mansion, you sonofabitch.

Cain realized what Matt was doing as soon as he reached for the rail gun. "Take cover!" And even as he screamed, he was suiting actions to words.

Matt picked up the rail gun and started firing into the troops.

Some of them dived for cover. Others tried to return fire. Even the return fire that did hit had no effect. Umbrella had done its work too well.

Matt had no idea who the prisoners were who had come with Alice, but one of them—the badly dressed black one who had been the only survivor back in the gun store—cried out, "Goddamn! He switched teams! *Go,* you big motherfucker, *go!*"

Even as he was cheering Matt on, Matt saw one of the guards standing over him take aim at Alice.

Matt was about to bring his own gun around to take

him out when another of the prisoners—the one in an Umbrella uniform; obviously he, like Alice, had switched sides—leapt up and took the guard out. He was now free of his cuffs.

So was the woman in the blue tube top. Both she and the Umbrella guy grabbed fallen weapons and joined Matt in firing on Cain's thugs.

"This is Cain, priority overload—initiate launch proceedings, effective *immediately!*"

He still couldn't see him, but Matt heard that bastard's voice all too clearly. He had ordered the missile strike. Raccoon City would be one big firestorm soon enough.

Then the stealth copter took off and started to chase Alice down.

She was staying one step ahead of them, but that couldn't last. Even Alice had her limits. So Matt ran over and grabbed the rocket launcher.

Then he turned and ran toward the building across from City Hall where the copter was chasing Alice.

By the time he caught up, Matt saw that Alice was defiantly facing off against the copter's bulletproof windows and 50 mm cannons with a Colt .45. Matt had to admire her tenacity, but even she couldn't beat those odds.

At least, not with that weapon.

With one mighty leap, Matt interpolated himself between the muzzles of the copter's cannons and Alice.

Then he raised the rocket launcher and fired it.

When Nemesis had blown up the inn on which the

S.T.A.R.S. sniper was positioned, Matt had wailed in agony as he was forced to watch himself kill a cop who had done nothing wrong but be stuck in a nightmarish situation.

Now, though, he took nothing but satisfaction from the task.

The copter exploded in a fiery conflagration.

He watched with peace of mind as the tail rotor broke away from the rest of the fusillage and plummeted down—

—right toward them.

Oh, shit.

As fast as he and Alice were, even they couldn't dodge the rotor—or the rest of the wreckage—in time.

Maybe it's better this way.

A fireball came crashing to earth, burying Matt in debris, burning metal, exploding fuel, and shattering pavement.

Now, at least, it's over.

THIRTY

Timothy Cain knew when it was time to retreat.

It seemed they would have to go back to the drawing board with the Nemesis Program as well. And he'd have to explain to his superiors why Charles Ashford hadn't made it out of Raccoon City alive. He would, of course, blame the good doctor himself, say that he'd managed to get back into the city somehow in a misguided attempt to rescue his little girl.

They'd believe that. Ashford was obscenely dedicated to that idiot child. The board of directors had even approved allowing the girl to serve as the template for the Hive's artificial intelligence avatar, a move that bewildered Cain no end.

Still, they had learned a great deal, and next time they wouldn't make the same mistakes.

Probably the most important thing was to find some

way to totally eradicate the personality of the host body for Nemesis. That had been the downfall of both parts of the experiment. Abernathy's individuality had proven too problematic, and even Addison had managed to overcome the programming.

It would also take a while to replace the troop leaders they'd lost. The soldiers themselves weren't an issue— such hired guns were a dime a dozen, easily found by combing armed forces, police departments, and jailhouses all across the world. They were near-infinite resources.

No, it was the men like Olivera, Ward, and One who would be difficult to replace. Along with Ashford, they were the only ones that Cain had anything resembling a regret about losing.

And even they could be replaced eventually.

Life, after all, was cheap.

He scrambled into the C89. Montgomery, the pilot, had already started up the copter.

Shouting over the sound of the rotor turning and the engine running, Cain cried, "Get us airborne!"

Behind him he could hear the exchange of gunfire between his own people and Olivera and that woman in the tube top, whoever she was. Based on what little he'd seen, she was a crack shot, as she and Olivera—whose skill Cain was already familiar with—were more than holding their own against almost a dozen of Cain's handpicked troops.

He also heard the woman yell, "He's getting away!"

No, he thought, he had already gotten away. He was going to survive, because that was what Timothy Cain did best. He survived everything the world had thrown at him, from the nightmare of going to high school as a newly arrived German immigrant to the perils of the Persian Gulf to these past few days in Raccoon City.

And he had not only survived, he'd thrived.

That was why he was the best.

He'd been standing in the cargo area for several seconds, but the copter hadn't moved.

Angrily, he walked to the cockpit.

"Why haven't we taken off?" he demanded.

" 'Cause I don't know what the fuck I'm doin'."

The voice was not Montgomery's.

The man in the pilot's seat turned around, revealing himself to be that black punk who was with Olivera and the woman in the tube top. For that matter, he'd been in the gun shop with the S.T.A.R.S. personnel, but, since he was very obviously *not* a threat, Nemesis had spared his life.

Cain realized now that that had been a tactical error.

Even as he reached for his Glock, the black man punched Cain right in the face.

Dazed, Cain fell to the floor.

"Little something I learned in grade school."

Cain's vision swam. He hadn't been coldcocked like that since basic!

He tried to get up, but he couldn't get his limbs to work. Dimly, he was aware of Montgomery's equally prone form next to him on the cockpit floor.

The next thing he knew, he felt hands grabbing him by the chest.

"Geddip."

That didn't sound right.

His vision cleared.

He saw the woman in the blue tube top. She had said, "Get up," he now realized. But he still couldn't make his legs move.

So the woman hauled him to his feet and pushed him into the cargo hold. The cold metal of a pistol's muzzle pressed into the flesh of his neck.

Blinking a few times, he saw Ashford's little girl standing in the hold, clutching a lunchbox, of all things, for dear life. Olivera was there, too, holding up Abernathy, who had a nasty wound in her chest.

That would heal, though. She was strong physically, even if she was weak mentally.

He wondered what had happened to Nemesis.

Now was the time for him to bargain. He could still get out of this.

"You have no idea what I could do for you. Don't make a mistake."

"Shut the hell up," Tube Top said.

From behind him, he heard the black man's voice saying, "Get us in the air, now! Don't make me hit you again, dog!" He was obviously talking to Montgomery.

"I could get you whatever you want," Cain said. "I could—"

Abernathy stared at him with her ice blue eyes.

Timothy "Able" Cain had faced the terrors of a desert war without fear. He'd come close to dying on hundreds of occasions. Not once during his entire tour was he ever scared.

Over a decade later, facing a lone, wounded woman in the cargo hold of a helicopter that was in the middle of a city about to be nuked, Timothy Cain was scared.

Saddam's troops had wanted to kill the enemy. It was nothing personal; they were doing their duty, as Cain had been when he killed them.

Alice Abernathy wanted Cain dead because he was Timothy Cain.

For the first time, Cain realized that life was not at all cheap. It was precious.

And he wanted to keep his.

"Please," he said. "What are you going to do to me?"

Alice pulled away from Olivera and walked over to him. She grabbed him by the shirt, just as Tube Top had.

"Not a goddamn thing."

Then she threw him out of the cargo hold.

He landed badly, but the damage was comparatively minimal. The helicopter hadn't yet taken off. He'd had worse in his time.

Now the C89 *was* taking off. Cain tried to get to his feet—

—but something grabbed him.

Even bulletproof material succumbs to enough pressure being put on it, and as good as Umbrella's new PlastiGlas was, even it would break if enough weaponry hit it.

Between the rail gun and the firefight between Olivera and Tube Top and his own people, the barriers that had kept the walking corpses from invading the square had collapsed.

Now they were coming in droves. And with the helicopter taking off, and the only other people in the square already dead, that left them with only one target.

Cain.

He fired on the one that grabbed his leg, then the one behind it. Both were head shots, which disposed of them right away, but that didn't change what was happening. There were hundreds of them—some of them his own troops, now revived by the T-virus that permeated the air.

Soon, Cain realized that he didn't have a chance. There were hundreds of them, and only one of him. This wasn't the desert; he couldn't count on the rest of his platoon—or reinforcements.

He was alone.

And he was going to die.

If that was the case, then he was at least going to do it on his own terms.

He put the muzzle of the Glock to his head.

Pulled the trigger.

It dry-clicked.

Out of ammo.

Then the corpse of Dr. Charles Ashford, complete with gaping bullet wound, grabbed him and bit him on the neck.

Timothy Cain screamed.

Others grabbed him and bit him, tearing the flesh loose from his body with their blackened teeth.

It took Cain a long time to die, and to learn just how cheap his own life had become.

THIRTY-ONE

Alice had never before enjoyed watching a person die.

But she took great glee in watching as a horde of undead swarmed over Major Cain and ate him alive.

Of all the things that Umbrella—that Cain—had done to her, this was probably the worst: they'd turned her into someone who could take joy from watching a person die horribly.

The helicopter took off, the pilot having been convinced of the urgency of getting the fuck out of Raccoon before they all died.

Alice, her strength spent, collapsed.

The rotor from the Darkwing that Nemesis—that Matt—had blown up had impaled her in the chest. She was lucky to be alive.

Or not, as the case might be.

Matt himself appeared to have been buried beneath the fiery remains of the stealth copter. Even if he was still alive, there was no way they could have gotten him out in time.

He was going to die when the missiles hit.

As she collapsed to the deck of the C89, she saw the contrails of the missiles as they came closer and closer to the city.

She hoped the C89 was faster than it looked.

Matt deserved better than this.

Hell, they all did, but Matt more than all of them. Except maybe Lisa, who at least had died quickly. Yes, she was then reanimated by the T-virus, but Alice had been able to do her the service of killing her quickly after that.

God. A service.

But all Matt had wanted to do was stop a corporation that had been reckless and illegal at best, murderous at worst.

She clambered farther inside the cargo hold, cursing Spence's name. If he had only waited one more day, Lisa would have given Matt the evidence of the T-virus, Matt would have leaked it to the press, and maybe the Hive would've been shut down.

And Raccoon City wouldn't be a ghost town.

It was only a pity she couldn't kill Spence a second time. Or a third.

The blood was still pouring from the wound she'd taken. Had she been ordinary, she'd already be dead, but even with her extraordinary new abilities, she didn't think she was going to last long.

She looked up to see Angie in one of the copter's seats.

Somehow, she managed a smile. "Buckle up, honey."

Angie looked scared to death but seemed to be holding up, despite everything. Alice wished she had the girl's courage.

"Are you going to be all right?" the child asked.

"I don't think so."

Alice could hear her own heartbeat.

It was fading.

The C89 had gotten beyond the city limits, but they were still a lot closer than Alice would have liked.

Carlos yelled out, "Hang on to something!"

Then she heard it.

The explosion was the loudest thing she'd ever heard.

It was the hottest thing she'd ever felt.

The C89 started tumbling, buffeted by the shock wave of the explosion.

Raccoon City, she knew, was now dead.

No, it was already dead. It had been dead from the moment Cain—that fool, that asshole, that fuckup—had ordered the Hive reopened. All the missiles did was perform the cremation.

Valentine cried, "We're going down!"

The copter tumbled through the air. Alice felt nauseated.

Then she saw a piece of the C89 rip off and fall toward Angie.

It was going to tear right into the girl.

"No!"

Gathering every erg of strength in her dying body, Alice leapt across the cargo hold and—

—just as Matt had done for her—

—put herself between Angie and the threat.

For the second time in ten minutes, Alice was impaled by a sharp piece of metal.

Perfect ending to a perfect day.

THIRTY-TWO

There were days when Dr. Sam Isaacs hated his job.

Right now, Isaacs longed for a day that good.

As he stood in his Hazmat suit watching the various technicians, also in Hazmat suits, check over the wreckage of the Umbrella helicopter that had crashed in the Arklay Mountains shortly after Raccoon City was wiped out, he thought on the one piece of good news he'd gotten all day.

Timothy Cain was dead.

True, Isaacs didn't actually rejoice in the fact that the man was deceased, but at the very least it meant he wouldn't be Isaacs's boss anymore. The man had been a complete imbecile with delusions of grandeur.

Worse, he'd had no concept of one of the most importants tenets of science, that of the *controlled* experiment.

Instead, he'd let the T-virus get out of the Hive—a nice controlled environment—and then he'd decided to use the killing fields of Raccoon City in the wake of this nightmare as the place to test the Nemesis Program.

It drove Isaacs crazy. Nemesis had been floundering for ages, and now they'd *finally* had a breakthrough. Abernathy and Addison were the perfect test subjects—Addison took to the mutations like a duck to water, and Abernathy had even taken it one step further.

Did Cain let Isaacs do his job and refine the process?

No, he'd let them loose in the city and set up some kind of idiotic death-cage match.

Now both subjects were as dead as Cain, and Isaacs would need to start over.

Not that that was the corporation's highest priority at present. After all, they had a serious amount of spin control to deal with. Isaacs didn't know how they were planning to manage that—blowing up a city wasn't exactly something you could brush under the rug—but that was hardly Isaacs's problem.

All he knew was that, based on the last report from Ian Montgomery before the pilot died in the crash, Cain was dead and Abernathy had been on this bird when it flew out of the city. If there was something—anything—to salvage, Isaacs needed it.

Then one of the techs moved a piece of wreckage to reveal Abernathy's entire body.

Intact.

Well, mostly intact—a large piece of metal had cut right through her thoracic region, but that could be removed. And studying her corpse would be extremely beneficial.

"Fetch the medical team," he said to one of the techs.

"Sir? She's dead, sir."

"Just do as I say." Save him from idiot technicians! "Any sign of any of the others?"

Another tech shook her head. "No, sir. There are charred remains in the pilot's seat—that was probably Montgomery. But there's no sign of *any* other remains. My guess is that Olivera, the two civilians, and the Ashford girl all made it out alive."

Isaacs shook his head.

"Unbelievable. The genetically engineered super-soldier doesn't make it, but the regular people and the little girl do?"

The tech shrugged. "It's a fucked-up world, sir."

"Crudely put, but correct." Isaacs sighed. "Keep checking. Just in case."

"Yes, sir."

Isaacs watched as the medical team approached and began pulling Abernathy's body from the wreckage.

Jill Valentine looked down on the wreckage from her vantage point atop one of the mountains.

She, Carlos, Angie, and L.J. had spent hours climbing this mountain, getting as far from the wreckage—and Umbrella's influence—as they could.

It was kind of ironic. For Jill, this whole thing had

begun in the forests not far from here, when she saw zombies.

When she'd reported it, Umbrella had worked overtime to discredit her and force her suspension.

Now she was back in Arklay. The city where she'd grown up, that she'd spent her whole life in, that she had sworn an oath to protect and serve, was gone.

Carlos, who was carrying Angie Ashford on his shoulders, said, "They'll be coming after us."

Jill reached into her jacket pocket.

"Their mistake."

Unlike last time, Jill now had evidence.

They couldn't brush this under the rug.

"Yo, can we be gone?" L.J. said.

Jill looked over at L.J. She wondered how this asshole had managed to survive when Peyton hadn't. L.J. was a cockroach.

But then, cockroaches had a way of surviving, too.

"Yeah, we need to get going. Besides, there's a lot of dead people who need someone to speak for them. Peyton. Angie's dad. Captain Henderson. Morales."

"Yuri," Carlos said quietly. "Nicholai. J.P. Jack. Sam. Jessica."

"Rashonda," L.J. added. "Dwayne."

"And Alice. And even Nemesis."

Angie spoke up then. "Alice isn't dead."

Jill and L.J. whirled on her, perched on Carlos's shoulders. "What?"

"Alice isn't dead."

"Honey," Jill said, "she was stabbed in the chest. I don't think—"

"I know what you think," Angie said emphatically, "but I *know* she's not dead."

Jill felt a shiver go up her spine. Partly at the notion that Alice had been *so* fucked with by Umbrella that even death couldn't stop her.

Partly because, if she was alive, she was still in the wreck of the C89.

Which meant Umbrella was going to find her.

THIRTY-THREE

". . . unconfirmed reports of disaster at Raccoon City . . ."

". . . These shocking images just in of diseased people walking the streets . . ."

". . . a mysterious plague or viral outbreak seems to have run rampant . . ."

". . . In an echo of the SARS outbreak in Central Asia and Canada, there appears to have been some kind of disease spreading throughout the city . . ."

". . . implicating the Umbrella Corporation in the death of innocent citizens as they attempted to escape the confines of the city over the Ravens' Gate Bridge. It is unknown at this time why Umbrella, rather than government authorities, was handling the screening of personnel, and why they would open fire on people. Some *are questioning why Umbrella even* has *an armed security force, while others feel that such questions are less relevant in light of subsequent events . . ."*

". . . tape apparently the work of former Raccoon 7 anchorwoman Terri Morales, who was moved to their meteorological department in recent months. The footage tells a grisly tale . . ."

". . . new evidence which discredits earlier reports as nothing more than a sick joke . . ."

". . . the fake videotape is now totally discredited. The woman responsible for filming the footage, Terri Morales, was removed from her anchor position at Raccoon 7 when she aired false footage of a city councilman, and it appears that this tendency of hers has continued . . ."

". . . nothing more than an elaborate hoax, playing on the very real tragedy which overwhelmed Raccoon City earlier this week . . ."

". . . the reactor of the nuclear power station went critical in the early hours . . ."

". . . making this the worst atomic energy disaster since the Chernobyl incident in 1986 . . ."

". . . Umbrella Corporation personnel actually on hand to lend humanitarian assistance in the face of the overwhelming human tragedy, despite the fact that the corporation itself suffered huge losses. Umbrella's primary corporate headquarters in Raccoon City were lost, as were almost a thousand employees . . ."

". . . governor has personally extended his thanks to the Umbrella Corporation for their swift actions in aid-

ing the FBI, the National Guard, and the Centers for Disease Control . . ."

". . . this station would like to apologize for the distress that may have been caused by the earlier hoax reports of a viral outbreak . . ."

". . . according to a spokesperson for the Umbrella Corporation, Terri Morales was within Raccoon City when the accident occurred, but the perpetrators of the hoax, Jill Valentine and Carlos Olivera, are now being sought for questioning by the FBI. Valentine is a former Raccoon City Police Department officer—in fact, she was part of the elite Special Tactics and Rescue Squad, or S.T.A.R.S., before she was suspended. The details of the suspension are not known, but a source with the Umbrella Corporation has indicated that it had to do with a similar hoax perpetration. As for Olivera, he is a former Umbrella employee who was let go shortly before the accident, and was last sighted at a cabin in the woods. It is possible that he holds a grudge against Umbrella, and was working with Valentine to discredit the company, with Morales as their unwitting dupe . . ."

THIRTY-FOUR

She woke up naked with the feeling that it had happened before.

But she couldn't remember when or how or why.

Or who she was.

She was in a tube, she knew that much. She was also all wet.

There was something on her face. Whatever it was, it allowed her to breathe underwater. Various tubes fed into her body, and she wondered if these tubes were providing her with food.

The upright tube she was immersed in was in a laboratory of some kind.

Two people were talking, one man, one woman. They were among the dozens of people in the laboratory, and the only ones whose words she could make out. She did not recognize either of them, though she felt she should. They both wore white clothing.

She didn't understand how she could know so much—like what a laboratory would look like—yet not remember so much more—like her own name.

The woman said to the man, "She's taking almost no nutrients from the system. The regen seems almost spontaneous. It's like she's sucking energy out of thin air."

She had no idea what any of that meant. Except for "thin air," which she assumed she had no access to, since she was surrounded by water.

The man looked at her. "Can you hear me? Do you understand what I'm saying?"

The thing on her mouth let her breathe, but kept her from talking. She remembered that nodding would work in this case, so she did.

"Good." The man turned to one of the other people in the laboratory. "Begin the purging process."

She heard a strange noise. Moments later, the water was down to her head—then her neck, her chest, and so on, until the tube was empty. Hot air blasted her for a few seconds, drying her off. Then the tube opened, and one of the people in the laboratory removed the tubes and the thing around her mouth.

Now she could walk around freely. She started exploring the room, taking in the sights, sounds, textures—the different colors of all the pieces of furniture and clothes, the humming of the various pieces of equipment, the coldness of the floor against her bare feet.

"Her recovery is remarkable." One of the people in white was talking about something—probably about her. "The regeneration of both organs and tissue is simply off the scale. And her powers, both physical and mental, seem to be developing at a geometric rate. Better than we ever could have hoped for."

One of the people in white—not the one who was talking—was sitting and using a stick of some kind on a piece of paper.

Another of the people in white, the one who seemed to be in charge of everything, asked, "You know what that is?"

She just stared at it—she had no idea.

The man in charge took it from the other man and started mimicking his motions. "Pen. See?"

He took her hand, put the stick—the pen, rather—into it and guided it onto the piece of paper.

"A pen," he repeated.

The man in charge let go, and she started using it on her own. She couldn't do much with it—even though she'd only just figured out what it was, she recognized that what she was doing with it was silly looking.

So silly, in fact, that she smiled.

"That's right," the man in charge said, "pen."

For the first time since they'd let her out of the tube, she tried to talk. "W—"

The sound came out scratchy. She tried again.

"Where—"

The man in charge prompted her. "Where are you?"

She nodded.

"You're safe. Do you remember anything? Do you remember your name?"

What was that?

"Your name?" the man in charge said again.

"Name?" she asked.

"That's right."

"My—name—is . . ."

The concept was tickling at the back of her mind. She knew what a name was, she was pretty sure, but it wouldn't come to her.

She sighed.

The man in charge turned to the other people. "I want her under twenty-four-hour observation. I want a complete set of blood work and chemical and electrolyte analysis by the end of the day."

Then, suddenly, it hit her.

"What's your story? The place is littered with ex-law-enforcement types who wound up here because it sucks everywhere else. There's got to be a story there."

"Don't judge a book by its cover. First rule of Security Division."

"I got where I am now by paying attention to things that nag me. So I just kept an eye on you. Then I noticed something."

"Once I realized that you and al-Rashan were coworkers and friends, it all came together. Pursuing a job with the same corporation that was all but responsible for your friend's death, to the point where you relocated from the city you'd lived in all your adult life, a

relocation you'd rejected six years earlier. Sure, there were circumstances to explain all of that—but not why you were so aggressively trying to get peeks at stuff you aren't cleared for."

"It's a T-virus, and you're right, it's not at all natural. Believe it or not, it came about from a study into something that would retard the aging process—a skin ointment that would keep the skin cells from aging."

"I can help you get the virus. I have access to security plans, surveillance codes, the works."

"Listen to me. I want to know who you people are, and I want to know what's going on here. Now."

"Kaplan, you've got to hurry, you've got to help them!"

"My God, Kaplan, there's something killing them in there!"

"You're not a cop, are you?"

"That homicidal bitch may be our only way out of here."

"Rain? Rain! We have to do something about your wounds."

"Kaplan—hold on! We're gonna come get you. We need to cut this wire, then we can throw it to him. Then we can go get him. Hold on!"

"Blue for virus, green for the antivirus. There's a cure."

"I was your sister's contact."

"Was that how you thought all my dreams were gonna come true?"

"I don't know what we had, but it's over."

"*The antivirus is right there on the platform—it's right there!*"

"*Rain, please, get up.*"

"*I'm missing you already.*"

"*Hey—no one else is gonna die.*"

"*I could kiss you, you bitch.*"

"*I failed. All of them. I failed them.*"

"*You're infected. You'll be okay—I'm not losing you.*"

"*My name's Alice. We're not safe in here. That fire will spread.*"

"*They hunt in packs. If there were more, we'd have seen them by now.*"

"*I used to work for them—before I learned the error of my ways.*"

"*It's nothing personal. But in an hour, maybe two, you'll be dead. Then, minutes later, you'll be one of them. You'll endanger your friends, try to kill them— maybe succeed. Sorry, but that's just the way it is.*"

"*Umbrella. They want to keep news of what's happening here from getting out.*"

"*They did something to me.*"

"*His daughter Angela is trapped within the city. We find her, and he'll help us escape the perimeter.*"

"*There won't be any help. According to Ashford, Umbrella knows it can't contain the infection. So at sunrise, Raccoon City will be completely sanitized.*"

"*He's dead. You can join him—or you can do as I say.*"

"*She's infected. On a massive level.*"

"They made me one of their little monsters."

"My name is Alice Abernathy. I worked for the Umbrella Corporation."

"I glimpsed hell, saw things I cannot describe."

"I became a freak."

"Sir!"

That was one of the lab techs—whose name, Alice now remembered, was Cole. He'd noticed something on the brain-wave pattern indicator and was trying to get the attention of the man in charge.

Dr. Samuel Isaacs.

The man who'd experimented on her and Matt Addison, at the direction of Major Timothy Cain, all for the benefit of the Umbrella Corporation.

Isaacs, though, wasn't paying any attention to Cole, or to Alice herself.

"Advanced reflex testing is also a priority. I want electrical impulses monitored and her—"

"Sir!" That was Cole again.

Sounding annoyed, Isaacs asked, "What *is* it?"

She didn't give him a chance to answer.

"My name is Alice. And I remember everything."

Isaacs went pale. He signaled one of the guards standing by the door, a young man named Doyle.

Before he could even draw his sidearm, Alice lunged at Doyle with the pen she still held, going for his eye.

Frozen in shock, Doyle didn't move, even though Alice stopped just a millimeter short of his cornea. The blow would kill him, after all, and Alice had no interest in killing a young man who was just doing his job. Besides, his wife was expecting a baby, and it wasn't fair to her.

Instead, she coldcocked him.

Two orderlies came out of nowhere to subdue her.

She subdued *them* in about two and a half seconds.

Then she grabbed Isaacs's arm.

Him, she wanted to kill. But, no, that wasn't fair—if he died, he couldn't begin to pay for what he'd done to her.

So she broke his arm. Let him feel pain for a while. It would *start* to compensate for the pain she'd suffered at his and Cain's hands.

Then she threw him headfirst into the tank she'd been held in.

A Taser dart hit her bare flesh and sent thousands of volts through her system.

She laughed. It tickled.

They had made her too good. So good that they couldn't stop her.

Ripping out the Taser dart, she threw it right back at the guard who had fired it.

He did not laugh. It didn't tickle him—though it did leave him insensate on the floor.

The other technicians, orderlies, and scientists fled the lab.

They were smart.

Down the hall, Alice knew—she wasn't sure how, but she *knew*—that a guard named Daellanbach was watching her on a surveillance camera and screaming into a telephone.

"This is Central, request immediate backup, maximum response. Nemesis experiment is loose—repeat, Nemesis exp—"

Alice wanted him to stop talking.

So he stopped, falling to the ground, nose bleeding, screaming in agony as something sliced through his mind.

Facing no resistance whatsoever, she left the lab and walked toward the front door. She was in Umbrella's corporate headquarters in San Francisco, which she now knew was where they'd relocated after the Raccoon City disaster.

She also knew that some friends were waiting for her in a parking lot outside, because she could feel the presence of one of those friends.

Angie Ashford.

Even though she had remained with Carlos and Jill, who were now fugitives, they had risked showing up here, because Angie knew that Alice would be here today.

Sure enough, an SUV was parked where she expected it to be. Carlos was driving, with Jill and Angie in the back.

"Where you been?" Jill said with a smirk. "We've been waiting all night."

"You took a big risk coming here," Alice said as she got into the shotgun seat next to Carlos.

"We like to live dangerously," Carlos said. "Angie said you'd be here, so we came. We figure you're worth the risk."

"Assuming," Jill added, "you can still do all those nice magic tricks you did in Raccoon City."

"And more," Alice said quietly.

Umbrella had thought that when they managed to cover up the Raccoon City disaster, it was over.

They were wrong.

Several lifetimes ago, Alice had approached Lisa Broward about revealing the existence of the T-virus to the general public in hopes of discrediting the Umbrella Corporation and forcing it to face up to its illegal, immoral activities.

Now Lisa was dead, Raccoon City had been destroyed, and Umbrella still rolled merrily along, believed by all and sundry to be a benevolent corporation.

Alice's determination to change that had only grown.

And the tools with which she would do it were the very enhanced abilities that Umbrella and its scientists had given her.

For them, the nightmare had just begun.

NOT THE END . . .

ABOUT THE AUTHOR

Born in the Bronx to a pack of feral librarians, Keith R.A. DeCandido is the best-selling author of dozens of novels, short stories, comic books, eBooks, and nonfiction books in a variety of media universes, ranging from *Star Trek* and *Doctor Who* to *Farscape* and *Gene Roddenberry's Andromeda* to Spider-Man and the X-Men to *Buffy the Vampire Slayer* and *Xena*. This is his second trip to the milieu of *Resident Evil,* following the adaptation of the *Apocalypse* prequel, *Resident Evil: Genesis.* His first original novel, *Dragon Precinct,* was published in summer of 2004, and he has several *Star Trek* novels in the works. Find out various uninteresting things about Keith at his official Web site at DeCandido.net.